ALSO BY KAREN E. QUINONES MILLER

Satin Doll

I'M
TELLING

A NOVEL

KAREN E.
QUINONES MILLER

SIMON & SCHUSTER
New York London Toronto Sydney Singapore

SIMON & SCHUSTER
Rockefeller Center
1230 Avenue of the Americas
New York, NY 10020

First Simon & Schuster trade paperback edition 2003

SIMON & SCHUSTER and colophon are registered trademarks
of Simon & Schuster, Inc.

For information regarding special discounts for bulk purchases,
please contact Simon & Schuster Special Sales:
1-800-456-6798 or business@simonandschuster.com

Manufactured in the United States of America

5 7 9 10 8 6 4

The Library of Congress has cataloged the hardcover edition
as follows:
Miller, Karen E. Quinones.
I'm telling : a novel / Karen E. Quinones Miller.
p. cm.
1. Self-destructive behavior—Fiction. 2. Literary agents—
Fiction. 3. Sisters—Fiction. 4. Twins—Fiction. I. Title.

PS3563.I41335 I4 2002
813'.6—dc21   2002021752

ISBN 0-7432-1435-8
0-7432-1436-6 (Pbk)

ACKNOWLEDGMENTS

I want to start by thanking my brother, Joseph T. Quinones, who has always been my rock. I may not say it out loud everyday, but I do thank you everyday, and I thank God that you're my family. I hope you know that I'll always be there for you, as you've always been there for me.

I would never have been able to complete this book without the support of Delin Cormeny (my old literary agent who has left the business), Liza Dawson (my new literary agent), Andrea Mullins (my old editor who has left the business), and Denise Roy (my new editor.) I really do need to try to figure why people who work with me over any extended period of time feel a need for a career change.

I also want to thank Hilary Beard, Jenice Armstrong, Kamal Rav, Mister Mann Frisby, and Sheila Simmons—the members of The Evening Star Writing Group in Philadelphia. I'm so proud to be a member—you guys are simply the best.

A big thank you to Karen Brown, Yasmin Coleman, Ladette Lima, and Katrina Love. I appreciate your input as I was writing *I'm Telling*.

There are so many people who have supported me, and I'm sure I'm going to blank out on a couple of names, but let me at least mention Beverly Moore, Al Hunter, Jr., Vaughn Slater, Karen Scott, Dana King, Bahiya Cabral, Pam Jones, Hanna and Hassan Sabree, Lorraine Ballard-Morril, William Banks of the Harlem Writers Guild, Sherlane Freeman, Keath "Lion" Lowry, Lisa LeVeque, Daaimah S. Polle, Helen Blue, Bobbi Booker, David Quinones, Belinda Cunningham, Estelle Cunningham, Daranice Miguel, Edwin DeVaughn aka BlacLov, Aunt Bernice, Deanna Corbett, William Thomas, Harold King, Cheryl Wadlington, Adrian Thomas, and Renee Thomas. I want to thank you all for believing in me.

I have to give a huge shout-out to the young princesses of the family. Charnell, Camille, Davina, Takia, Toni, Taice, Maniamah, Chloe—all of you are so very precious to me.

And a remembrance to those who transitioned over the past year—Ted Holiday and David and Mary Curry.

Big thanks to the book clubs that have supported me and other African American authors: Circle of Sisters, Rawsistaz, Journey's End, Eye of Ra, Diva's Den, Escape Book Club, African Jewels, Sistahs On the Reading Edge, Pure Essence, Shades of Color, Sistah Time Book Club, 4 the Love of Books Book Club, Black Novel Book Club, EDM Book Club, Circle of Friends Book Club, Sisters Are Reading Book Club, Page Turners Book Club, Sistahs Book Club—you are all so wonderful and so appreciated by me. I especially want to thank those amazingly supportive and energetic women of the United Sisters Book Club, who were the first group to have me read an excerpt from *I'm Telling*, and The Sisters Uptown Book Club, who've always made me feel welcome and at home.

I have to thank the book store owners who have been so sweet, encouraging, and supportive. Andre and Kim Kelton of Our Story, Sherry McGee of Apple Book Center, Emma Rodgers of Black Images

Bazaar, Stacy Foster of Kujichagulia, Janifa Wilson of Sisters Uptown, Lloyd Hart of The Black Library, Trust Graham of Nubian Heritage, Larry Cunningham of Culture Plus, Frances Utsey of Cultural Connections, Malita McPherson of Heritage Books, Adline Clark of Black Classics Books and Gifts, Haneef and Haneefa of Haneef's Book Store, Felicia Winton of Books For Thought, Nia Damali of Medu Bookstore, Michele Lewis of the Afro-American Book Stop, Brother Simba of Karibu, Robin Green-Carey of Simbanye Book Store, Betty Liguorius of Liguorious Books, and Scott Wyth of Reprint Books.

I've met so many other authors who have been very supportive and loving. I'm glad to call you colleagues and friends—especially Gloria Mallette, Mary Morrison, Eric, Pete, and Zane. Thanks guys!

And last, but certainly not least, I want to thank my daughter, Camille Renee Quinones Miller, who has been a true gem. I still can't believe how lucky I am to have such a wonderful child. Thank you, Love Girl . . . for everything.

Maferefun Olodumare
Maferefun Oshun
Maferefun bobo Orisha

I lovingly dedicate this book to Kitty—my other half

I'M
TELLING

PROLOGUE

I squeezed my eyes real tight, but I couldn't get what I had just seen out of my mind. My stepfather's face in between my twin sister's legs. Even with my eyes closed I could still see them. And I could smell them, too. A funny smell. Kind of like sweat and something else. And I could hear them whispering and scrambling around like they were trying to grab up their clothes. I kept my eyes shut and squatted down in the corner of the bathroom, covering my ears and clenching my teeth so hard they hurt.

I wanted to run downstairs and hide under the blanket in my bed, but if I did, I would have to run past the bedroom door where I had just seen them doing the nasty.

"Faith? What are you doing up here?" I heard Papa call to me, real quiet like.

I bit my lip and cursed to myself. I was kind of hoping that we could just keep on playing the game that we'd been playing for about a year. Me knowing that him and Hope were doing bad things when Mommy wasn't around, but pretending I didn't. Well, I didn't know

1

exactly what they were doing, but I knew they were doing something. That's why Hope had become Papa's favorite all of a sudden. Not that I cared about that so much, about him having a favorite. I never did like Papa, not from the very first time Mommy brought him to meet us, when me and Hope were seven years old. My big brother, Allen, liked him all right because he taught Allen how to talk to girls. And my little brother, Johnny, liked Papa, too, because Papa took him to baseball games. But me, naw, I never did like him. There was something about him.

Hope took to him right from the very beginning, though, always hugging and kissing him good night. Then last year, just after me and Hope turned ten, I noticed that they were hugging and kissing a whole lot more and a lot longer. Something wasn't right about it. They started spending a bunch of time together, and they whispered to each other a whole lot when they didn't think anyone was looking. I was always looking, though, because I was the big twin and all my life everyone always told me it was my job to look after Hope. I hated it when I saw him rubbing her shoulders and touching her face and all that, and I hated the way she giggled when he did that stuff. I wanted to tell, but I didn't really have anything to tell. I mean, I knew something was going on, but I didn't know exactly what. I thought about asking Hope—we always used to share secrets—but I was afraid of what she might tell me if I did. Instead I just kept my mouth shut. I guess I really didn't want to know.

So if Hope and Papa were in the room together and I needed to get in for some reason, I would stomp real hard on the floor when I was walking so they could stop whatever it was they were doing before I came in. Because I knew they were doing something. I know they knew why I was doing all that stomping, I know they did. And so it was like we had some kind of a deal. I didn't do anything to try and catch them, and they didn't do anything too bad right in front of me.

But dang, dang, dang, how come all of a sudden they didn't close the dang door before they started doing the nasty? And especially since Mommy was right in the house. Right downstairs. But no, not even when I came stomping up the stairs to get to the second-floor bathroom. When I saw Mommy's bedroom door open, I thought everything was cool, else I would never have turned my head when I passed to get to the bathroom. Papa looked up from in between Hope's legs just as I turned my head, and we looked straight dead into each other's eyes before I could run past.

"Faith?" Papa's voice seemed more uncertain this time, and for a minute I thought about not answering him. Maybe he would think it was just his imagination, my walking past. But then I heard him whisper to Hope to go in the bathroom and see if anyone was in there. I wouldn't have been able to stand that, looking into my twin's face and having her see in my eyes that I knew what she had been doing.

"Yeah, it's me, Papa," I called out quickly. I stood up and walked to the bedroom doorway as if nothing had happened. I was thinking maybe we could go back to the game. Maybe I could pretend I really didn't see anything.

"What are you doing upstairs?" Papa's shirt was off, but he was pulling up his pants. Hope was standing next to the bed, looking down at the ugly green shag carpet, not saying anything. I got really mad when I saw she was wearing a yellow dress. Mommy always bought us the same style dress, but in different colors. Hope's dresses were blue, and mine were yellow. Hope was wearing my dress while doing the nasty with Papa.

"What are you doing here?" Papa asked me again.

"Mommy said for me to get her pocketbook so I could go get some brown sugar from the store because she's going to surprise you with a pineapple upside-down cake for your birthday and we didn't have any brown sugar so I'm supposed to go to the store to get some, but I had to get Mommy her pocketbook so she could give me the money so I could go to the store but she said she left her pocketbook in the upstairs bathroom, so she sent me upstairs to get it for her so she could send me to the store to get the brown sugar." I was talking so fast I was out of breath. I peeked up from the floor at Papa when I finished talking, but then I looked down again real quick. His zipper was open and part of his thing was hanging out. Eeww. I don't think he realized it, though. He was staring at me real hard, like he was trying to figure out something to say.

"Okay, I'm going to get Mommy's pocketbook so I can go to the store. Bye!" I ran to the bathroom and snatched up Mommy's black patent-leather pocketbook off the dirty clothes hamper, and I was ready to run past the bedroom and down the stairs, but Papa stood in the bathroom doorway.

"Look, Faith, you don't have to tell your mother everything you know, okay?" Papa was talking real slow, like he was picking his words real careful like. "And get yourself whatever you want while you're at the store. I'll tell your mother it's okay."

I could feel tears come all the way down from my brain to my eyes, and I tried real hard not to blink, because I didn't want to be crying. But why couldn't he just have pretended that he didn't know I had seen them? Now he went and said that, and that meant I would have to tell Mommy, because if I didn't, we would all be playing another game—one called "Let's All Hurt Mommy." And I didn't want to play that game. And even if I did, he might go ahead and decide that since I was playing he could do the nasty with me, too. I didn't put it past him, because he was such a nasty old man. And Hope was nasty, too, because she was doing the nasty with him. But if I did tell Mommy I would be telling on Hope, and I never told on Hope and she never told on me. Not ever. But then again, if I did tell, Mommy would put Papa out, and that wouldn't be such a bad thing. But then Mommy would be all sad because even though she was real pretty and real smart and went to college and everything, she was real fat, and she probably wouldn't be able to get another man to like her. And then Mommy would be back trying to support me and Hope and Allen and Johnny on the pay she got as a bookkeeper in the real estate office on 116th Street. And she would cry at night like she used to before Papa started coming around. And it would be all my fault for telling.

"Okay, Papa," I said real quite like as I walked around him. "I'm going to the store now."

"Okay. And be a good girl."

I could feel his eyes on me as I walked down the hall. I heard the door close when I was halfway down the stairs. Back to finish what they were doing, I guess. But even through the closed door, I could hear my twin ask, "Do you think she's going to tell?"

I sat on the bottom step and put my face in my hands. But I was too confused to cry.

1

"Shit!" Faith stumbled back from the greasy cabinet door as a large mouse scurried from behind the two-pound box of Uncle Ben's rice for which she had been reaching.

"What did you say?"

"Nothing, Mommy," Faith hollered from the kitchen into her mother's bedroom. The rice was unopened, but she inspected the packaging carefully to see if it had been assaulted by the fleeing mouse. It hadn't.

"Yes you did. I heard you say something," came Miss Irene's teasing reply. "And don't you be cursing in my house. You may be thirty and a hotshot literary agent, but I'm still your mother, and I can still get up off this bed and put a foot in your behind."

"Twenty-nine, Mommy."

"What?"

"Nothing."

"What did you say?"

"Nothing," Faith hollered again.

"Yes you did. I heard what you said. I'm your mother and I know how old you are. You're thirty years old. I don't know why you have to keep lying about your age," Miss Irene hollered, before bursting into laughter.

Faith grunted and looked around the tiny kitchen for something to wipe her hands with. She picked up a hand towel that was thrown over the back of a rickety wooden chair, but threw it back down when she realized it had large, black mildew spots on it and smelled. Ugh.

She used to come over and clean up for Mommy, but gave up when she realized that Mommy didn't care one way or the other and that the house would be back to its same nasty state in a matter of days. Faith once thought that Mommy had had a nervous breakdown a few years back and somehow this accounted for her wanting to live in utter filth. The house was never like this before Papa left Mommy for a younger woman. Faith even once suggested that Mommy see a psychologist, but her mother flew into a rage. It had to be some kind of neurosis; no normal person could actually want to live in a pigsty—especially someone who prided herself on her personal appearance, like Mommy did. What was even more amazing was that Mommy's sometimes live-in boyfriend, Ronald, didn't seem to care about the filthy conditions either. But then he didn't seem to care about much besides figuring out where he was going to get his next drink. He seldom made it home before the bars closed.

Faith gave up and wiped her hands on the back of her olive green wool skirt. Thank goodness she hadn't worn anything fancy, although she still wished she had thought to bring an apron to cover the skirt and light-green knit turtleneck sweater. Mommy always said she and Hope should avoid green—that the color was unflattering to their skin tone. She had listened when she was younger, but discarded the fashion advice in her late teens after her boyfriend—Henry—bought her a fabulous green suede coat with a golden lambskin collar. It was the first of many expensive gifts he lavished on her over the years. The coat was a size twelve, and she was a size ten at the time, but she didn't care. Now, ten years later, the coat (which had long since been donated to The Salvation Army) would perfectly fit her mature body. At five feet four inches and 140 pounds, with breasts so firm she seldom wore a bra, Faith had a small waist and a big butt that drove men wild. She loved buying clothes now as much as she had as a teenager, and with her growing business as a literary agent she could well afford the expense. But she still enjoyed getting lavish gifts, and Henry still enjoyed giving them. She pushed her auburn, shoulder-length hair out of her face and licked her full lips as she thought about the floor-length golden beaver coat that Henry had bought her the day before. She had thanked him properly that night and looked forward to thanking him again when he returned from Chicago in a few days.

God, I hope they finish this deal soon, she thought. Being an investment banker, Henry had to frequently take trips to evaluate the financial stability of companies that his firm was considering investing in. He'd been traveling back and forth to Chicago for the last month or so, to assess a small publishing company that in two years had managed to put out four books later grabbed up by larger publishing houses and turned into *New York Times* best-sellers. It was one of the few times when Henry's line of work and Faith's actually intertwined.

She turned down the flame under the heavy metal saucepan and threw in a handful of diced onions and bell peppers, which sizzled noisily in the hot olive oil. She reached inside the counter drawer, ignoring the sprinkling of brown roach eggs, pulled out a can opener, and opened a can of tomato sauce to add to the oil and vegetable mixture. Then she added two tablespoons of salt, a dash of black pepper, garlic powder, and oregano—and the kitchen began to fill with a spicy aroma. She searched briefly for a measuring cup, then finally gave up and went to the sink full of dirty dishes and washed a Skippy peanut butter jar. She filled it with Uncle Ben's rice and dumped it into the saucepan, followed by two peanut butter jars of water. She covered the saucepan, wiped her hands on her skirt once again, and headed out of the makeshift kitchen and into her mother's adjoining bedroom.

The whole house had at one point been converted into kitchenettes or efficiency apartments, as had so many brownstones in Harlem during the Great Depression, when people needed cheap rental space to live and homeowners needed extra money to pay their mortgages. Mommy rented out the second and third floors of the brownstone and kept the basement level and most of the first floor for herself—and whichever one of her kids needed a place to stay at the time. At the moment that was Hope, since Allen had moved in with his girlfriend the year before and Johnny was still in the army. Faith had been the first of the children to leave the house, departing at age sixteen because of her hatred for Papa. She didn't even return for visits until after he moved to Brooklyn with his new woman, who was one-third his age.

The basement level had a full kitchen and two bedrooms. The first floor once contained an enormous parlor, a small coat room, a dining room, and a small bathroom. Miss Irene, though, turned the parlor into a bedroom that she sometimes rented out, converted the coatroom into a tiny kitchen, and turned the dining room into a combination bedroom and living room for herself. Pushed to the left corner of the large room was an ashwood captain's bed, from which the four-hundred-pound Miss Irene seldom strayed. Next to the bed was a badly chipped mahogany night table, upon which sat a brand-new 32-inch color television and VCR. In front of the television was an aluminum folding chair, reserved for anyone who stopped by to say hello. In the middle of the room sat a rickety brown couch with urine-stained cushions that one of the tenants had dragged in from the street. A sagging triple dresser and chest of drawers hugged the wall, along with a computer desk that was covered with old papers, but no computer. The computer Faith had bought her mother a few months before had been stolen by one of the tenants, which really didn't matter since her mother had never used the thing.

"Mom, I'm going to have to make you a steak instead of pork chops." Faith pushed aside the dirty laundry, including smelly underwear that had been thrown on a raggedy armchair—once gold, but now brown with dirt and age—and sat down.

"Why's that?" Miss Irene, clad in a gray housedress, size fifty-two, lay on her side, her salt-and-pepper hair pulled back into a bun and her brown-rimmed glasses perched on her nose. People meeting her for the first time would always say, "She's so pretty to be so big." She had golden brown skin, with large slanted eyes, and a light smattering of freckles around her nose. Her hands were small and dainty, like those of a young child. Her nails were always meticulously manicured and polished.

"Why can't you make my pork chops?" Miss Irene asked again.

"No mustard," Faith replied, gearing up for an argument.

"But I had my mouth all fixed for your delicious pork chops," Miss Irene whined. "Can't you just run to the store real quick?"

"Mom, come on. It's pouring down rain outside, and it's freezing. Can't you just eat steak?" Faith whined back.

"Why do you need mustard for pork chops?"

Faith had forgotten the presence of Tina, also known as "Third Floor Front," after the space she occupied in the house. Faith didn't like the woman, whose face was sunken and skin an ashy gray. Like most of Mommy's tenants, Tina was a crackhead and was always coming up with excuses about her rent being late.

"It's a special way we fix them. We season them with vinegar, salt, black pepper, and garlic powder," Miss Irene explained to Tina, who sat on the aluminum chair facing Miss Irene's bed, "then we spread mustard on both sides, dip them into flour, and fry them."

"I've never heard of it. I guess it's good?"

Faith rolled her eyes. She knew what was coming next.

"It's delicious. You've got to try some," her mother answered, while enthusiastically licking her lips.

"Well, I tell you what, I'll run to the store for mustard if you make me one of those pork chops." Tina turned to Faith with a smile that revealed yellow teeth thickly covered with plaque.

"Nope." Faith looked Tina straight in the eye, daring her to say anything else, but Tina looked away and got up as if to leave the room.

"Faith, why do you always have to be so evil?" Miss Irene glared at her daughter before turning back to soothe her favorite tenant, who seemed to be near tears. "Tina, don't worry. I'll make you a pork chop myself if you'll run to the store for me."

Yeah right, Faith thought, but said nothing as she waited for Tina's reply.

"No, that's all right. I'm really not that hungry anyway," Tina said, as she wiped her runny nose with her coat sleeve. "But I'll go to the store for you anyway, Miss Irene. You're always so nice to me, it's the least I can do."

Faith rolled her eyes but said nothing. That's what the crackhead witch should have offered in the first place, she thought.

"Thank you, sweetie. Let me give you some money." Miss Irene sat up and reached for a white envelope that lay on the corner of the night table. She handed Tina a ten-dollar bill.

"I don't mean to be a bother, but could you hurry up? It smells like the rice is almost done." Miss Irene faced Tina as she spoke, but looked at Faith out of the corner of her eye.

Faith noticed the signal and obediently walked Tina through the kitchen to the front door.

"Now, you know if you don't come right back with my mother's change I'm going to kick your ass again, right?" Faith crossed her arms and stared after Tina, who hurried out the door in silence.

Faith had nearly reached her mother's bedroom when she heard the unlocked front door fly open. She whirled around, fists clenched, thinking that Tina had found some backbone.

"Hey beautiful!" Hope grabbed her around her neck, almost knocking her down with enthusiasm, and planted a big wet kiss full on her lips before Faith could get a word out. Faith shivered slightly from the cold rain on Hope's coat sleeves. "Long time no see, Baby Girl! Where you been hiding and stuff?"

"Nowhere, Baby Girl. And stop yelling!" Faith grinned as she always did when she saw her bubbly, energetic twin sister. They looked almost exactly alike, although Hope was just a shade lighter, which to enough people meant that Hope was the "pretty" twin. Faith noticed that Hope had also dropped a little more weight. She was getting downright skinny.

"I know, I know, I talk loud and stuff," Hope said with no apology in her voice as she grabbed Faith's hand and pulled her toward their mother's bedroom. "Anyway, whatchoo cooking? I can smell it all the way from outside."

"Is that what made you finally bring your butt home after two days?" Miss Irene looked at Hope and sucked her teeth. "The least you could have done was call and say you were okay."

"I know, I know, I'm inconsiderate and stuff. Whatchoo up to, Mom?" Hope leaned down and kissed her mother on the cheek.

"Look what I bought ya," she said as she dipped her hand into her coat pocket.

"What's this?" Miss Irene smiled with delight as she turned over the small silver contraption in her hand.

"It's a tape recorder, Mommy! See, it takes little, tiny tapes," Hope said, pointing to a minuscule compartment on the front of the recorder.

"It's a micro-cassette recorder. I have one of those," Faith said with a laugh. "Hope, what is Mommy going to do with one of those?"

"I don't know. There was some guy selling it hot for five bucks on Malcolm X Boulevard, and it looked like something Mommy would like and stuff, so I bought it," Hope shrugged. "If she doesn't want it, you can have it, I guess."

"No, she's going to have to buy her own. This one's mine!" Miss Irene's eyes gleamed as she turned the small recorder in her hands over and over again.

"Like I said, I already got one. And y'all should both be ashamed of yourself buying hot items off the street." Faith sniffed the air, then ran into the kitchen. "Oh, shoot, I have to turn off the rice."

"Don't pay her any mind, sweetie, you know she's a snob. You just keep buying your Mommy these nice gifts," Miss Irene said as Hope sat in the aluminum chair and clicked on the television to watch music videos.

"No, you guys really should stop. You know darn well that the guy you bought that from probably stole it from someone. You're supporting theft," Faith said as she returned to the bedroom. She looked back and forth at the two of them—Miss Irene still gushing over the tape recorder and Hope trying to look wide-eyed and innocent as if she really cared about what Faith was saying.

"Oh forget it," Faith said finally, plopping back down into the armchair.

"What did you tell Tina when you walked her to the door?" Miss Irene asked, finally putting the tape recorder down on the bed beside her.

"Just what you wanted me to tell her," Faith answered. "I told her she'd better get back here with your money quick or I was going to hurt her."

"Good. I wanted to make sure she didn't run off with my money."

"Baby Girl, you so mean," Hope said, though her eyes never left the television screen. Her favorite show, *Wheel of Fortune*, was on. "You know Tina is scared to death of you since you beat her up last time you were here."

"I only did it because of you and Mommy," Faith protested. "It's not like I care about that crackhead one way or the other."

"Well, she deserved it," Miss Irene said solemnly. "I know she was the one who took my twenty dollars out of the night table. And then for her to threaten Hope after she confronted her about it—well, she needed someone to show her that she can't get away with treating people like that."

"But see, Mom," Faith leaned forward in the chair, "then you can't understand why I get upset when I come back and she's right up here in your face again."

"Well, you already taught her a lesson," Miss Irene said defensively. "Besides, she's good company. You know she has a—"

"A master's degree from Yale," Hope and Faith said simultaneously.

"She's still a thieving crackhead, though," Faith added dryly.

"And a liar, too. You know last week she went and told Ma that she saw me in a crack house and stuff? I wanted to beat that crackhead's butt myself," Hope huffed.

"Uh huh, except you know she would have beat your butt and you would have to call Faith to fight your battles again," Miss Irene teased.

"I ain't call Faith to beat Tina up last time. You did!" Hope protested loudly.

"'Didn't call.' Not 'ain't call.' Why do you have to use such bad grammar?" Miss Irene snapped. "And how many times do I have to tell you that you sound downright stupid using 'and stuff' in every other sentence. Why can't you talk more like your sister?"

"'Cause I *ain't* my sister," said Hope, pouting. "And I don't be hearing you getting on Allen and Johnny 'bout the way they talk."

"Your brothers don't talk anywhere nearly as badly as you!"

"Well, then good for them!"

"Look, all I'm saying is that it doesn't make sense for you to have me push Tina around one day, if you're going to have her sitting watching television with you the next," Faith continued as if she didn't hear the bickering between her mother and Hope. "I'm not going to come running next time you call me and tell me that Tina did something to you, Mommy."

"Oh shut up, Baby Girl, you know you will." Hope got up from the chair and playfully swatted Faith on the top of her head. "That's what you do best."

"Yeah, when I was fifteen." Faith shook her head. "I'm twenty-nine now, and I have a reputation and career to think about."

"Thirty," Miss Irene said.

"Twenty-nine!" Hope and Faith said together.

"C'mon Mommy, we ain't gonna be thirty until June and stuff," Hope snapped at her mother. She then sucked her teeth and sat back down in the chair facing the television, but looking at her mother out of the corner of her eye.

"Well, you're closer to thirty than you are to twenty-nine, so you might as well as say thirty," Mommy snapped back. "And don't you suck your teeth at me. I'm still your mother, you know."

"Well, I'm staying in my twenties until the very last moment,"

Faith broke in before Mommy and Hope could get going on yet an-other fight.

They'd been like that since the twins hit puberty—Miss Irene and Hope, going through tandem mood swings. One moment they were sharing gifts and fawning over each other, the next they were verbally tearing at each other's throats. Usually it was Hope buying the gifts and Miss Irene starting the arguments, but the roles occa-sionally reversed. Both would call Faith on the telephone to give their side of the story, as if she really gave a damn. It was *their* crazy relationship, let *them* deal with it. The only time Faith got involved was when the arguments started in her presence and Miss Irene started hitting Hope below the belt. Faith couldn't stand by and let anyone abuse her twin for long—not even their mother.

Not that Hope didn't have her own stuff with her; some of the things she did to Miss Irene were downright despicable. But that was a whole other issue.

"Hey, how's Mrs. Trumble?" Faith asked.

"She's okay. Well . . . actually, she's not." Hope turned her com-plete attention to her sister, ignoring her mother, who still looked like she wanted to argue. "I'm gonna go and check on her inna little bit and stuff. I think she's got pneumonia, but she won't go to the hospital."

"Why won't she go?" Faith asked.

"Because she's stupid," Miss Irene snapped. "I don't know why you keep going over there and waiting on that woman hand and foot, Hope. It's not like she pays you or even appreciates it."

"She's an old lady, Mom. I think she's something like eighty-five years old," Hope shrugged. "And I don't know why you always got to make it like I'm there all the time and stuff. I just wanna stop by from time to time and make sure she's okay."

"Why do you have to do it?" Miss Irene asked.

"She ain't got no kids or anything, Mom. Who else is gonna do it?" Hope asked in an exasperated tone.

"Man, you are such a sweetie." Faith shook her head in wonderment at her twin. When they were kids, Hope played nursemaid to the wounded dogs and cats in the neighborhood. As she got older, she started checking in on the older folks on the block—accompanying them to doctors' appointments, running to the store for them, and reading them the newspapers. And no matter how much they insisted, Hope would never take a dime from her charges. People are supposed to help other people, she would say.

"Hope's a dummy, is what she is," Miss Irene said meanly. "She takes better care of that old woman than she does of her own mother."

"Mommy, that ain't true," Hope said plaintively. "I'm always doing stuff for you."

"What's that?" Miss Irene looked around the room trying to locate the faint sound of music.

"My cell phone!" Faith raced over to the coat rack in the corner of the room and pulled her cell phone from a pocket, all the while chastising herself for leaving valuables in the same room as crackhead Tina. She hit the send button to answer the call just as the last strains of Scott Joplin's "The Entertainer" faded away. Damn. Missed the call. She hit the caller ID button and her home telephone number appeared. Henry's back?

"Your cell phone plays music?" Miss Irene asked incredulously.

"Yeah, ain't that neat?" Hope grinned.

Faith waved her hand at her mother and sister, signaling them to keep the noise down as she hit the return call button. "Hey, lover! What are you doing home from Chicago?" She twirled a strand of her hair as she smiled into the telephone. "I thought you weren't going to be back until Wednesday. Did something happen?"

"Hey, Princess," a soft baritone voice answered. "The head of the publishing company had to cancel our meeting because his wife went into labor. When I found I flew out there for nothing, I hopped on the next flight home. You know I had to come home to my baby."

"Mmm . . . and you know your baby loves the fact that you're home?" Faith turned away from Miss Irene and Hope, both of whom were giggling and making kissing sounds as she talked. "Are you going to have to make another trip out there, then?"

"Yeah, I'm flying back out the day after tomorrow." Henry stifled a yawn. "Are you at your mom's?"

"Mm hmm. I'm fixing dinner for her tonight, remember?" Faith stepped on a cockroach that was scurrying across the floor in front of her. "Why don't you come over and join us?"

"No, I think I'll pass. The Knicks are playing the 76ers tonight so I thought I'd catch the game." Henry yawned again. "What time do you think you'll be home?"

"Around ten or so."

"Cool. I'll be here waiting for you, baby. I love you, Faith."

"I love you, too, Henry."

"Mmm, good . . . that's what I needed to hear. Let me speak to the Queen Mother before we hang up, baby."

Faith dutifully handed the cell phone to Miss Irene. "Your boyfriend wants to speak to you," she rolled her eyes, but was unable to suppress her smile.

"Stop acting so jealous." Miss Irene grinned as she took the telephone. "Hi Henry. How was your trip? . . . Oh, I'm sorry to hear that. . . . Did you bring me back anything? . . . Really? . . . Oh, goodie! I've always wanted one of those! . . . Can you bring it over tonight? . . . Oh, okay. . . . Not until next week? . . . Well why don't you send it over by Faith if she can stop by here sooner? . . . Okay, then sweetie. . . . And don't forget. . . . Alrighty then, Henry . . . bye." She switched the telephone off and handed it back to Faith. "Henry bought me one of those computerized Spanish/English translators!" she said excitedly.

Faith sighed and shook her head wearily. "And why would he have bought you something like that?"

"Because he adores me, of course." Miss Irene grinned. "And I might have mentioned that I saw a television commercial for one and really wanted it."

Hope rolled her eyes. "He never buys me anything."

Faith shrugged her shoulders. "You're not always begging him for gifts like Mommy is."

"I beg your pardon!"

"I was only kidding, Mommy," Faith said soothingly. "But you have to admit, you are always trying to con him into buying you things."

"No, I don't. He just likes pleasing his almost-mother-in-law," Miss Irene huffed.

"When are you guys going to get married anyway, Baby Girl? Ya'll been together for like twenty years now an' still ain't tied the knot and stuff."

Faith glared at Hope. Now why does she want to say something like that in front of Mommy? she thought. Her mother had been bugging Faith about getting married for years, saying that she should threaten to leave Henry if he refused to set a date. Miss Irene wouldn't believe Faith when she told her that it wasn't just Henry. Neither one of them was in any rush. Things were going as great now as when they were lovesick teenagers. They did plan to marry . . . eventually. They talked about it from time to time. They even went and got a marriage license every January for the last ten years, so if they wanted to get married on the spur of the moment they could. That was Henry's idea. He was always coming up with crazy notions like that.

"Well, at least you're going to get to play bridesmaid even if you don't play bride. I can't wait until . . . oops!" Hope hurriedly covered her mouth with her hand, a guilty look spreading over her face.

"Play bridesmaid, what are you talking about?"

"Huh? Oh, nothing and stuff . . . I was just . . ."

"Miss Irene? I'm back." Tina appeared in the bedroom doorway, dripping wet with two small brown paper bags in her hand. "I'm sorry, I thought it would be okay to come in without knocking since the door was open and I had just left anyway," she said when she saw the look in Faith's eyes.

"You always coming in here without knocking," Hope said with a laugh, "why you apologizing now?"

Tina ignored the question. "I stopped at the liquor store while I was out and bought some brandy—out of my own money," she said handing both bags to Faith with a hopeful grin. "I figured we could all use a shot to keep warm."

"I'll pass." Faith took only the smaller bag, then looked inside to make sure it contained the mustard. It did.

"I want some!" Hope leapt to her feet. "Where's the glasses and stuff?"

"Tina, I wish you had brought Manischewitz Cream White Concord. You know I prefer wine, but I guess I can drink some brandy. There's some plastic cups in the dresser drawer," Miss Irene said. "I try to keep them handy so I don't have to keep going back and forth to the kitchen if someone needs a glass," she said when she saw Faith's head shaking in disapproval.

"Oh, Miss Irene, I almost forgot!" Tina said after Hope handed her a cup. "Mrs. Crawford from down the street was in the grocery store. She asked me to let you know that Oprah was going to be rerunning the show she did with Sidney Poitier tomorrow."

"Really? Oh, Hope, make sure you set the VCR up for me!" Miss Irene clapped her hands in delight, causing Tina to chuckle.

"You must really like him," she said to Miss Irene.

"She loves him. And Harry Belafonte, too." Hope laughed. "Ooh, ooh, I got one for you, Mommy!" she suddenly hooted. "I can't believe we didn't do this one before. Faith, come here . . . I got a good one." She pulled her sister over so that they were both standing directly in front of Miss Irene, who looked at them expectantly.

"Sidney Poitier or Harry Belafonte? Which one would you choose?" Hope demanded.

Faith leaned a little to the side, put her hand on her hip, and thought for a moment. "Ooh, that is a good one. I can't believe we didn't do them before . . ." she cocked her head and looked at her mother who was struggling with the question. "Mommy, we haven't done this one before?"

"You know, I don't think we have. This is a hard one," Miss Irene answered slowly. "They're both handsome, though in different ways. They both have sexy accents. But I think I'm going to pick Sidney Poitier because he's a better actor . . ."

"But Harry Belafonte can dance! I used to love watching him swing them hips and stuff," Hope chimed in.

"Mm hmm, and I love his voice," Faith added enthusiastically.

"You're right!" Miss Irene nodded her head in agreement. "I'm going to go with Belafonte."

"Me too!" Hope said.

"I'm going with Poitier," Faith said after a few more seconds of thought.

"Why?" Miss Irene asked in a shocked voice. "You just said you love Belafonte's voice."

"Yeah, but remember when I was seven and Aunt Gloria took me to do some back-to-school shopping on 116th and Park Avenue and we saw Sidney Poitier down there?" Faith wiggled her finger between her mother and sister, who listened intently to find out why Faith had broken ranks. "Well, remember he patted me on the head and bought me an ice cream cone just because he said I looked like one of his nieces."

"Oh, that's right," Hope said slowly. "You know what? I change my vote."

"How are you going to change your vote now?" Miss Irene demanded. She sat up straight on the bed, put her hand on her hip, and glared at Hope. "You and I both said we liked the way Harry Belafonte shakes his hips, don't change up on me now because Sidney Poitier patted your sister on her head."

"Well, I'm not changing it for the pat on the head, but I kinda think buying a kid an ice cream deserves two votes and stuff," Hope said with a shrug.

"Traitor!" Miss Irene scowled at Hope, causing the twins to start giggling.

"Well, I'll side with you, Miss Irene." The three women had been so caught up in the little game that they had forgotten about Tina, who stood waiting—impatiently, judging by the tapping of her foot—for them to pour the brandy Miss Irene had placed on the night table.

"It's a family thing, your vote doesn't count," Faith said. She instantly regretted the harshness in her voice. After all, the woman had gone to the store to buy the mustard. And she was even treating to brandy. Faith retreated to the gold armchair and Tina quickly stepped in front of Miss Irene with plastic cup in hand.

"Thanks anyway, Tina," Miss Irene said as she poured a bit of brandy into Tina's cup. "And I really think it's time we address the inimical feelings so evident in this room."

"What's 'inimical'?" Hope asked as she held a plastic cup out toward Miss Irene.

"I beg your pardon?" Miss Irene raised an eyebrow at Hope.

"What does 'inimical' mean, Mommy?"

"You don't know the definition of 'inimical'?" Miss Irene said in a shocked voice.

"It's not a word that's used in everyday language, Mommy." Faith frowned. She knew what her mother was doing and didn't like it one bit.

"I wouldn't say that," Mommy said. She returned the brandy to the night table and then positioned herself comfortably on the bed. "Tina, you know what 'inimical' means, don't you?"

"It means hostile," Tina answered. Faith could see that she was trying to hide a smile as she spoke.

"Well, I ain't never heard of it, and I don't consider myself no dummy and stuff," Hope said defensively.

Faith grimaced, preparing herself for her mother's next comment, which was sure to be barbed. She wasn't disappointed.

"It just shows you what a failure the New York public school system is," Miss Irene addressed Tina with a haughty wave of the hand. "To think a child could go through twelve years of education and not know the definition of 'inimical.'"

"Mommy! Why you gotta go there like that?" Hope looked crushed, but Miss Irene ignored her.

"Well, some might say it's the failure of the public school system, others might say the failure is on the part of the child's parents," Faith said in her snootiest voice. "And after all, not everyone was as fortunate as you and Tina, who had parents that *cared* enough to send their children to private schools."

Miss Irene struggled back to a sitting position and leaned forward as if to confront Faith's snide remark, but then seemed to think better of it. Instead she just glared at her.

"Come on, Baby Girl. I'll keep you company in the kitchen while you fix her pork chops." Hope pulled Faith up from her chair.

"Ooh, you got Mommy back good." Hope chuckled as soon as they were out of earshot. "I bet the only reason she didn't say anything else to you was because she thought you'd put rat poison in her food or something."

"Oh come on, I'd never do anything like that!" Faith protested. Hope pursed her lips, crossed her arms, and looked at her twin sister.

"Well, okay, I did it once before. But that was only to Papa, and it wasn't rat poison, it was roach spray," Faith said grudgingly. "And it doesn't count because he didn't die."

2

Gin and tonic, please—with a double twist of lime."

Faith reached up and disentangled one of her teardrop diamond earrings from the collar of her light-golden-colored full-length beaver fur while pretending not to notice the four men gaping at her from across the dimly lit bar.

The barmaid politely took her order, but Faith could see the glint of curiosity in her eyes and knew the woman would try playing twenty questions with her when she returned with the drink. The smell of fried chicken coming from a back kitchen, the old grease-spotted unframed portraits of celebrities on the walls, and the chipped tiles on the floor confirmed that The Renaissance Lounge was a neighborhood hangout, not a snazzy nightclub. Women dressed like Faith didn't usually park themselves on bar stools at The Renny.

Faith slipped off her cream-colored leather gloves, placed them on the stool next to her, and unhooked her coat, which opened to reveal a gold satin sheath dress. She looked over her shoulder to locate the ladies' room and noticed someone just slipping in, so she unsnapped her cream-colored leather clutch, pulled out her compact, and quickly checked her makeup while still sitting at the bar. Flawless—as was her hair, which was pulled back into a French braid. She snapped the compact shut and replaced it in her clutch just as the barmaid placed her drink on the bar in front of her.

"Do you take American Express? I'd like to run a tab." Faith pulled out a gold card and flashed it at the woman.

"Sure." The barmaid looked as if she wanted to make conversation, but she was suddenly called to fill a drink order from a customer farther down the bar.

Faith took a sip of her gin and tonic. Watered down. She wasn't surprised. She twirled the stirrer for a moment before glancing up at the mirror over the bar. Two women seated in a booth were glaring at her. Both were about her age. One was wearing a decent-looking brown leather coat. The other was wearing a fake mink, which probably looked a lot more genuine before Faith stepped into the joint.

Still staring in the mirror, Faith turned her attention back to the group of men at the other end of the bar. One was an older guy in his sixties with short salt-and-pepper hair, who looked like a college professor in his suit and tie and horn-rimmed glasses. Next to him was a thirty-something-looking man dressed in construction gear. On the other side of the professor were two guys wearing security guard uniforms. Faith licked her lips and swiveled her barstool toward that end of the room. The two security guards looked away quickly, as if they didn't want her to catch them staring. The professor caught her eye and smiled. She ignored him and stared at the construction worker, who seemed lost in thought as he peered down at his bottle of Heineken.

He was dark-skinned, with thick eyebrows and a small, neatly trimmed mustache. He had a slim build, but even sitting down he was obviously tall. A black knit cap covered most of his hair, which looked to be a medium-length Afro. His dark-brown down jacket was opened, revealing a flannel red-and-black plaid shirt. Beige thermal underwear peeked out from behind the shirt's open collar. Huge dark brown gloves, speckled with paint and plaster, lay on the bar next to his beer. He looked as if he'd just finished a hard day's work. Mmm, he looks good, Faith smiled to herself.

It was a few seconds before he looked up, but when he did, Faith leaned forward on her stool and mouthed "Hello" to him. She had to suppress a giggle when the professor almost dropped his drink. The man in the construction gear looked at her in surprise for a moment, then simply nodded and looked back down at his beer.

Well, I'll be damned. Faith blinked in disbelief. He's actually going to play hard to get. This should be interesting! she thought.

She signaled to the barmaid, who hurried over.

"Would you please send another beer over to this gentleman here in the wool cap?" she asked, pointing to the man, who was obviously pretending not to notice. "And tell him I'd be pleased to receive an invitation to join him."

The barmaid paused as if to assess her sincerity, causing Faith to flash her an annoyed look that sent the woman scurrying.

Faith watched the man's face carefully as the barmaid presented him with the fresh drink and enticing message. Disbelief seemed to be his initial reaction—he looked at the waitress, the drink, at Faith, then back to the waitress. The professor seemed to have overheard the waitress's message because he, too, became animated, poking the construction worker in the side with his elbow as if urging him to take some kind of action. The construction worker finally picked up the Heineken and tilted it in Faith's direction as if in salute, then took a sip and placed it back down on the bar. The professor flashed a wide, silly grin at Faith, then turned toward the construction worker and seemed—from his facial expression and body language—to berate the man. The construction worker looked at him coolly, took another swig of his beer, and said nothing.

Hmmph! This had better be worth all the hassle I'm going through, Faith thought as she picked up her gloves, clutch, and drink and headed down the bar. The professor's back was turned toward her, but the construction worker could see her as she approached.

"Hello. I hope you don't mind if I interrupt." Faith stepped in between the two men's barstools, smiling pleasantly as she spoke in a sultry voice.

"No, not at all." The professor quickly moved his seat to allow more room. "I was hoping you'd join us."

"Really? How nice," Faith responded to the professor while looking directly into the construction worker's eyes—he seemed to be searching her eyes in return. She tried to fight the unexpected blush that was creeping up from her neck, and found herself lowering her eyes to avoid his stare. This seemed to amuse him, and when Faith looked back up, she saw that his thick eyebrows had relaxed and he was wearing a half-smile that made him look all the more sexy. Now that she was up close, Faith could see his deep-set eyes and rugged masculine features. He smelled of expensive cologne, not one that a person would think a construction worker might wear.

"Thank you for the drink." His voice was clear, with a slight bass.

"You're very welcome," Faith answered as she lightly touched his arm. It was time to pull herself together and get back in charge of the situation. She moved closer to him.

He smiled a knowing smile as he watched her hand brush his bicep. He cocked his head and started, "My name is—"

"Shh!" She pressed the index finger of her free hand against his lips to stop him from speaking, then smiled into his eyes, leaned in, and lightly kissed the finger, brushing his lips with her own as she did so. "It's really not your name that I want."

She could feel his breath quicken. Good, she thought. I'm finally getting somewhere.

"Well, then, what is it you want?" he asked in a husky voice.

His legs were opened wide on the barstool and the bulge in his pants almost made her lick her lips in anticipation. She stepped closer to him so that she was actually between his legs and almost in physical contact with his crotch.

"I very much want . . . what I think . . . you very much want . . . to give me," she said slowly as her finger circled his mouth.

"Oh, God damn!" a male voice cried out behind her.

Faith had completely forgotten about the security guards and professor and was caught off guard by the exclamation, but she had enough presence of mind to keep her eyes focused on the seemingly mesmerized man in front of her. She leaned toward his ear and said in a loud whisper, "I have a hotel room just ten minutes away. Are you interested?" She flicked her tongue over his earlobe.

"Yeah!" was all he managed to say.

"Good!" Faith pulled back and turned to the bar while continuing to brush and occasionally squeeze and fondle the man's arm.

"I'd like to settle my tab," she told the barmaid, who was staring at her mouth.

"Sure." The barmaid scribbled down a figure on two checks and placed one down in front of Faith and the other in front of the construction worker.

"I'll take care of both of these." Faith handed over her credit card. She fastened her fur coat, pulled the collar up over her neck, and slowly pulled on her gloves, her eyes never leaving the construction worker's face.

"Ready?" he asked after she signed the bill.

"I can't wait for you to find out just how ready I am." She tucked her hand into the crook of his arm and snuggled close to him as they walked to the door.

"Oh sweet Jesus in heaven, why the fuck did she pick him instead of me?" she heard the professor say just before they left. She looked up at the construction worker to see if he had also heard. The huge grin on his face indicated that he had.

"So, you're really not going to tell me your name?"

"I'm really not going to tell you my name." Faith smiled at the construction worker as they stood in the middle of the hotel room sipping the white zinfandel that she'd had waiting for her return. The taxi ride to the Sheraton had been short and the two had done very little talking. He did offer to pay the taxi fare, which she thought was a nice touch, but she declined.

"Well, what should I call you?"

"Whatever you'd like." Faith laughed lightly and leaned into his body. He smiled and kissed her on the top of her head, but then pulled away.

"So do you do this often, I mean, pick up strange guys in bars and take them to hotel rooms and all?"

"Not often." Faith took another sip of her wine and stepped back to reappraise her conquest.

"But often enough?"

"What do you mean?"

"Well, you don't seem the least bit nervous."

Faith laughed, placed her drink on the mahogany writing table, and walked to the sliding glass door that led to a balcony overlooking the city. "Why? What are you planning to do to me?" she teased.

The construction worker chuckled as he placed his empty glass next to hers, walked over, took her in his arms, and squeezed her tightly.

She turned her head up and kissed him softly on the lips, then flicked her tongue around his lips and mustache, then lightly trailed it to his ear lobe, which she then gently sucked.

"Damn, you're so sexy." He was breathing heavily and massaging her shoulders as she began to lightly kiss down his neck to his upper chest.

"I have another question." He pushed her slightly away.

"Now what?" she threw her head back and moaned.

"If you don't tell me your name and I don't tell you mine, how can we get in touch with each other after tonight?" he asked in a reasonable voice.

"We don't," she answered just as reasonably.

"What?" He stepped back, still holding her by the shoulders, and looked at her as if in shock.

"Look, why are you making such a big deal out of this? Why can't you just lay back and enjoy? I thought this was every man's dream— a night of unbridled sex with no hassles and no commitments," Faith said in an annoyed tone.

"Yeah," the construction worker said slowly, "but what if I like it and I want more?"

"See? Now you're being greedy. Why not just enjoy tonight and think about what great memories I'll be leaving you with," Faith teased, moving back toward him and playing with the buttons of his shirt.

"So, it's like that? You just want to be a mystery woman?" he asked as his breath once again began to quicken.

"Isn't a little mystery a good thing from time to time?" Faith placed her arms around his neck and kissed him on the chin.

"I'm not complaining. I just find you, and all of this, very interesting." He started caressing her hair, then roughly grabbed her and pulled her toward him for a long, smothering kiss.

The abruptness of it caught Faith by surprise, and she instinctively tried to pull away, but he held her fast and she felt her body instantly become aroused in response to his sudden and unexpected passion. His hands firmly rubbed up and down from the back of her neck to her butt, causing her dress to rise above her panty hose. She threw her head back and moaned as he slid one of his hands into her panties and began squeezing the cheeks of her ass.

He moved his head closer to her neck and began kissing and nibbling her neck and shoulders, causing her unrestrained nipples to harden. Then he slid the hand that was in her underwear from her behind to her front, and then down between her legs, forcing the lips of her vagina open and expertly rubbing her clitoris.

"Hmm . . . you're all wet and juicy," he whispered in her ear. "You want it pretty bad, don't you, Mystery Woman?"

Faith was gasping, trying to catch her breath—everything was happening so fast and feeling so good. She tried to open her legs wider to give him greater access, but was restrained by her panty hose. As if sensing the problem, he picked her up with one hand—the other was still exciting her clitoris—and threw her onto the bed, her dress around her waist.

He knelt on the bed beside her and again kissed her deeply, then placed his free hand firmly on her chest, pinning her down as he thrust his finger deep inside her. She let out a small scream and lifted her hips, inviting him to go deeper. Instead, he took both hands and jerked her panty hose down from her hips to past her knees, then pulled one leg from the nylons, and then the other.

He stood up—still fully clothed—and looked down at her lying on the bed, half-nude. "Will you look at that?" he chuckled. She felt a moment of embarrassment and attempted to pull her dress down, but he caught her hand, stopping her.

"Don't start getting shy on me now. This is what you wanted, isn't it?" he asked gruffly. Then he reached down and grabbed the back of her head, pulling her to a kneeling position on the bed. Still standing, he kissed her again, then reached behind her with both hands and ripped her satin dress down the seam, leaving her totally naked.

The savagery both excited and frightened her, and she pushed both her arms against his chest, trying to get away.

"What's the matter, baby? Don't you want me anymore?" he asked, then grabbed her wrists with one hand and yanked her arms over her head. He then began kissing her neck, working his way down to her breasts. He licked around one of her nipples and then flicked his tongue over it before taking it in his mouth, sucking and softly nibbling on it. Faith writhed in ecstasy, her hands still pinned together over her head. He moved to the next breast and did the same.

"Oh, God, please," Faith moaned, her head swinging wildly from side to side.

"Please what?" he asked as he again began kissing her neck.

"Please fuck me. Oh, God, please fuck me. You're driving me crazy." She was almost crying as she spoke.

"Am I?" He chuckled. "You like it a little rough, don't you, Mystery Woman?"

He finally released her arms, and she immediately grabbed him around the neck, kissing him all over his face. He pushed her down, then pulled her by the knees until her legs were hanging off the side of the bed and her crotch was at the end of the mattress. He stared down at her expectant face and then slowly began unbuckling his pants. Faith shuddered in anticipation as he dropped his pants and pulled down his white briefs to reveal his large, throbbing penis. He bent over her and, balancing himself on the bed with his elbow, began kissing her neck and shoulders, causing her to once again moan and writhe. He started rubbing her breasts before moving down to her stomach and finally between her legs. She let out a gasp as he started playing with her clitoris and fingering her opening. He licked her ear lobe and then whispered, "Do you still want me, Mystery Woman?"

"Oh, God, yes," she moaned loudly. "Oh, please, yes."

She moaned even louder as she felt him direct his hardness to the lips of her vagina. He then rubbed it over her slippery clitoris and placed it at the tip of her opening.

"Oh, please give it to me," she pleaded as she lifted her hips in an unsuccessful attempt to force him inside of her.

"Mmm . . . are you sure you want it?" he asked, his breath was as heavy as her own.

"Oh, God, yes."

She let out a small scream of delight as he slowly pushed the tip of his organ inside her. She again thrust her hips up to take more of him, but he pulled back with her thrust.

"Oh, no, please don't tease me," she moaned.

"I'm not teasing you. I just want to make sure you want it." He began kissing her, still maintaining his position inside of her.

"But I want you. I told you I want you. Oh, God, I want you so bad." She began kissing him all over his face, moaning all the while.

"Good." He stuck his tongue inside her mouth as he pushed another inch inside her.

"Oh, yes. Oh, please, yes. Oh, please, do it. Oh, please, give it to me. Please." Faith's head shook wildly from side to side and her arms flew up and down his bare back as she begged.

"Open your eyes and look at me," he commanded. When she

complied, he slowly started moving inside her—bringing himself almost all of the way out, then gradually easing himself back in, but never farther than the few inches he had already penetrated.

"Mmph!" Faith gasped involuntarily. "Oh, God, it's so good."

"You like it, baby? You want more?" He kissed and licked her neck while massaging her breast and continuing his slow and deliberate movements inside her.

"Oh, yes, please, give me more!" she almost screamed.

"See? Now you're being greedy. Why not just enjoy what you have? He lifted his head and looked directly into her half-glazed eyes as he spoke.

"Huh?"

"You don't mean that something could actually be so good you might actually want more, do you?" he asked, then eased another inch inside, causing her to let out another wild moan. He once again began his erotic movements, driving her crazy.

"Yes, I want more. Please give me more. Please, I want more!" Faith begged, tears streaming down her face. Her heart was pounding wildly, her blood racing, and she couldn't control the writhing of her body or the moans escaping her throat. She was ready to explode, but every time she was just on the brink, he would slow his movements.

"No, baby, you're being greedy now. But don't worry, you'll have great memories of tonight, right?"

"What are you talking about? Please stop teasing me. Please fuck me all the way," Faith sobbed. "I'll do anything you want. I'm begging you. Please!"

"Tell me your name!" he said, suddenly quickening his pace.

"What?" Faith moaned. She was right there. Right there. She was going to climax in just another second.

"Tell me your name, now!" He stopped his movements completely.

"Faith! My name is Faith! Please don't stop now!"

"Faith what?"

"Faith Freeman!"

He rewarded her by slowly pushing inside another inch.

"Where do you live, Faith Freeman?" he asked as he resumed his movements.

"409 Edgecomb Avenue," she said without hesitation.

He pushed inside a little more, moving even faster. Her moans had turned to pants and he could tell she was getting ready to come.

"What's your—"

"555-1826!" she shouted.

He grabbed her by the shoulders and gave a mighty thrust, burying himself inside her to the hilt. Her body froze for a moment, as if in shock, then she let out a scream as the pleasure overwhelmed her, forcing an explosive orgasm to escape. Through the fog she could hear him calling her name over and over again as he also reached his climax.

Oh, my God, she thought. This is so wonderful.

They lay in each other's arms for a few minutes, catching their breath, then he propped himself up on his elbow and smiled down at her.

"You know I love you, right?" He kissed her on the forehead.

"You know I love you, too, right?" she answered softly.

"Yeah, I know." He kissed her again and stood up.

"Where are you going, Henry?" Faith asked lazily.

"To get my mystery woman a glass of wine." He smiled.

"I can't believe you got me to tell you my name," she said as she propped herself on her elbow and watched him move across the room.

"Yeah, well, when you're good, you're good. And I'm damn good." He began beating his chest.

"Oh, shut up!" She threw a pillow at him. Henry caught it and threw it back at her, causing them both to start laughing. He poured them each a glass of wine, then walked over and pulled down the bedspread at the head of the bed and patted the mattress for her to join him.

"Sexy, sexy, mystery woman." He sighed as she snuggled in his arms. "Faith, you know you had that guy at the bar going, didn't you? You should have heard him telling me I was crazy not to buy you a drink when you first smiled at me."

"Did he?" Faith laughed. "I could tell he wanted me."

"Yep. Those other two guys, too. They were playing it cool, but they both were talking about how you looked like you'd be a tiger in bed."

"Hmm . . . and you played so hard to get I had to end up looking like a bitch in heat," she said as she played with the hair on his chest. "It would have served you right if I had given up on you and left with one of those other guys."

"Then you would have missed out on all this." Henry took Faith's hand and placed it over his limp organ.

"And you would have missed out on all this." Faith took his hand and placed it between her legs.

"Tell you what, next time we role play, I'll pick you up, and you can play as hard to get as you want."

"Fair enough." She yawned. "This room is comfortable. Maybe we should go ahead and stay the whole weekend."

"Works for me." Henry yawned back. "Do we need a wake-up call in the morning?"

"You have somewhere you need to be?"

"Nope."

"Then we don't need a wake-up call." She snuggled closer in his arms as he pulled the bedspread further up their bodies.

"Did I mention that I love you, Faith Freeman?"

"Yep. Did I mention that I love you, Henry Prince?"

"Yep."

"Then go to sleep." Faith closed her eyes and was about to drift off when she heard her pager, which she had placed on the night stand, go off. She lifted her head up to look at the clock radio—2:00 A.M. She pulled the bedspread up over her head and waited for the beeping to stop.

"Babe, you're not going to see who's paging you?" Henry asked sleepily.

"No. I'll check in the morning." The beeping finally ceased, and Faith once again started drifting off. As if on cue, the pager started beeping again. She groaned.

"Babe." Henry shook her.

"I'm asleep," Faith mumbled from underneath the covers.

Henry reached over, picked up the pager, and looked at the number.

"Faith, get up. It's your mother's number."

"I said I'm asleep," she said, still underneath the covers.

"Faith, get up." He shook her urgently. "She put a 911 behind her number."

Faith quickly threw the bedspread off and reached for the pager as if to verify Henry's statement. Henry passed her the cell phone, which was also on the nightstand, and she quickly punched in her mother's number.

"Mom, it's me. What's wrong?" she said when her mother answered the telephone.

"Have you heard from Hope?" Miss Irene asked in a teary voice.

"No! What happened? Is something wrong?"

"I caught your sister in bed with Ronald today." Miss Irene started sobbing on the telephone. "They were right in my house, in the next bedroom."

"Oh, Mommy, are you okay?" Faith's shoulders sagged. Poor Mom. What the hell is wrong with Hope? she thought. Henry put his arm over her shoulder and asked in a whisper if everything was all right. She nodded her head and returned her attention to her mother.

"Oh, I'm okay. I threw that little bitch out, though," Miss Irene snapped.

Faith closed her eyes and inwardly sighed. She didn't bother to ask if she had thrown Ronald out, too. If Mommy hadn't thrown Papa out for screwing Hope when she was eleven years old, she wasn't throwing Ronald out now that Hope was twenty-nine.

"You know she's going to be trying to move in with you because I'm certainly not going to let her back in this house after what she's done," Miss Irene continued.

"Well, I haven't heard from her yet. What time did all this happen?"

"About an hour ago."

"Well, she'll probably call me in the morning. I'll call you back then, okay?"

"You don't have to call me and tell me anything about her. As far as I'm concerned she's not my daughter." Miss Irene started sobbing again.

"Mommy, you want me to come over?"

"No, I'm okay. You go ahead and get some sleep. Just call me tomorrow to make sure I'm okay."

"Are you sure? I really don't mind. I can be there in fifteen minutes."

"No, Ronald's here, and he and I really need to talk and work this thing out."

Throw your daughter out but work it out with the guy screwing her? Faith paused to regain her composure before speaking again.

"Okay, I'll give you a call tomorrow, Mommy."

"Okay, sweetie. I love you."

"I love you, too."

"What was that all about?" Henry asked when she hung up the telephone.

"You don't want to know." Faith sighed and handed him the phone, which he replaced on the nightstand.

"Yes I do," he insisted.

Faith sighed again and then lay down on the bed, pulling the bedspread over her body. "Mommy caught Hope in bed with Ronald."

"With whom?"

"With Ronald. You know . . . Mommy's boyfriend."

"Oh. Damn." Henry paused for a moment, then shrugged his shoulders and lay back down beside Faith. "So how many of your mother's boyfriends has Hope screwed now?"

"I think this makes three. Four if you count Papa." She snuggled against his chest.

"Wanna go to breakfast in the morning, babe?"

"Sure, why not?" she said as she drifted off to sleep.

"Goddammit, Irene, I told you I'm finished talking about it!" Papa slammed his fist down hard on the kitchen table. "I said I'm sorry. What else do you want me to say?"

Faith looked at her sister, sitting, playing with her Barbie dolls, trying to make believe that she couldn't hear the conversation—couldn't hear Papa cursing and Miss Irene crying. Didn't she feel the least bit guilty? Faith wondered. She knew she did, and she wasn't the one who had done something bad. Or had she? Telling Mommy was the right thing to do, wasn't it? And she had waited until Allen and Johnny were out of the house, when she and Mommy were alone in the kitchen. She had even waited until Mommy had put Papa's birthday cake in the oven 'cause she didn't want to bother Mommy while she was busy mixing the batter.

"But, Alfred, we've got to talk about it." Faith peeked out of her room and down the hall where she could see her mother had started crying again. She'd been crying all afternoon, her eyes were so red and puffy that it looked like she had a bad cold.

"She's my daughter. My eleven-year-old daughter." Mommy blew her nose and looked up at Papa with those hurt, sad, red, and puffy eyes.

"Irene, I know she's your daughter. And I said I'm sorry. I don't know what got into me, okay?" Papa stomped over to the window and stared outside at the trees, which were just beginning to sprout little baby leaves. Faith crept out of her room and stood right outside the kitchen door to get a better view, making sure Mommy and Papa didn't see her. She still couldn't believe that Mommy was the one crying and Papa was the one that was mad. Shouldn't it be the other way around? And why hadn't Mommy called the police?

"Damn it, Irene, how many times do you want me to say I'm sorry?" Papa was still staring out the window and he sure didn't look sorry to Faith. He just looked mad. Like he wanted to hit somebody. Faith tiptoed back into her bedroom, just to make sure it wasn't her. Hope was still sitting on the floor playing with her Barbie dolls, a strange look pasted onto her face. Faith shivered, suddenly feeling the cool evening air that was blowing the sheer pink curtains she and Hope had just put up the day before.

"Hope . . ." Faith was only going to tell her sister that she should close the window since it was getting cold, but she stopped when Hope looked up at her. There was a look of pure terror on her sister's face. Her eyes were wide and tearful, but they spoke to Faith, pleaded with Faith, "Please don't ask me about it. Please don't make me talk about it." The look startled Faith, and she unconsciously started backing up, not knowing what to say. She suddenly noticed that the pile of dolls lying on the floor were both naked and headless.

"You stupid little bitch!"

Faith hadn't realized that she had backed into the hallway until she bumped into Papa, who then knocked her into the wall so hard she saw bright flashes of light dancing in front of her eyes.

"You should be watching where you're going instead of minding other people's business!" Papa raised his hand to hit her, and Faith was too dazed to duck, but Mommy was between them before he could strike.

"Alfred! Leave her alone!"

Papa's hand came down across Mommy's face—hard. Mommy screamed and backed into the wall, covering Faith.

"You fat bitch! After all I've done for you and your kids you're going to take her side against me? You would have lost this damn house if I hadn't paid your back mortgage when I moved in," he yelled as he hit her. Faith ran to the kitchen and grabbed the receiver from the wall telephone and dialed 911.

"Police! Please come help my Mommy—" was all she could get out before Papa grabbed her from behind so forcefully that the telephone was pulled from the wall.

"MIND YOUR FUCKING BUSINESS! THAT'S ALL YOU CAN DO IS TELL EVERYTHING YOU SEE, ISN'T IT?" Papa was shaking her so hard that her head jerked back and forth and she could feel her brain banging from side-to-side against her skull.

"ALFRED! NO!" Mommy let out a scream so loud the walls seemed to vibrate. For some reason the scream worked, and Papa let go of Faith, who hurriedly scrambled into a far corner, out of his reach.

"It's your fault!" Papa snarled at Mommy who was crawling toward him. "You picking your kids over me, after all I've done for you? No one but me would ever hook up with your fat ass. Look at you! You look like a beached whale. You can't even get up off the floor."

Mommy braced herself against the wall and tried to rise up from the floor, but collapsed back down, her face enveloped in tears.

"You want me to leave? You want me walk out of your life right now? 'Cause I'll do it, you know!" Papa yelled at her. "I'll pack my shit right now and I won't look back. Then see how you do! You want me to leave?"

"I never said I wanted you to leave!" Mommy started blubbering. "I love you, Alfred, you know that. I don't want you to leave!"

"Then why are you giving me such a hard time?" Papa demanded as he stood over Mommy. "I told you I was sorry about what happened with the girl and you can't just leave it at that? I told you it wouldn't happen again, didn't I?"

"No, you didn't," Mommy managed to get out. "You said you were sorry, but you didn't say you wouldn't do it again. That's all I wanted to hear. I didn't want you to leave. And I wasn't going to throw you out. I just wanted you to promise it wouldn't happen again."

Papa stood silently for a moment while Faith huddled in the corner and Mommy sobbed on the floor. "Come here, baby," he finally said, and reached down and helped Mommy to her feet. She buried her swollen face in his shoulder, whimpering as he patted her back. "I'm sorry, baby. I don't know what got into me, and I swear it'll never happen again. You believe me, don't you?"

Mommy sniffed and nodded, her head still buried in his shoulder. Mommy's back was to Faith, so she didn't see Papa mouth at Faith, "I'm going to get your little ass."

It was too much for Faith, who sobbed and then ran past them into her room where she saw Hope, tearless but wide-eyed, yanking yet another head off a Barbie doll, seemingly oblivious to everything that had transpired. Faith collapsed on her bed and cried into her pillow. It wasn't until *the next morning, when she and Hope were getting ready for school, that she noticed that the headless naked dolls all had blue ink on their stomachs. When she looked closer, she saw that the pelvic area on each one had been viciously mutilated with the pen.*

"Faith, baby, wake up! You're having a nightmare!"

"What? What?" Faith's heart beat wildly, as if she had just finished a marathon. She sat up in the bed. "What? What happened?"

"I don't know! You started screaming in your sleep." Henry pulled her to his bare chest. "Are you okay? What were you dreaming about?"

"I don't know," Faith stammered. "I don't even remember. But I know it was scary."

"Okay, okay, baby. It's okay. Try to go back to sleep," Henry said soothingly as he rubbed her back. "And just remember, I'm right here with you. No one can hurt you, because I'm right here, okay?"

"Okay." Faith yawned, then settled into Henry's arms. Within minutes she drifted back to sleep.

3

"And what are you doing sneaking into the office on a Sunday morning?"

Faith jumped at the sound of an unexpected voice greeting her as she entered the fifth-floor office on 125th Street in Harlem. She patted her chest to slow her rapid heartbeat when she realized it was just her partner, Ann Swanson, sitting at a mahogany desk and sifting through a large stack of papers.

"Random House was supposed to fax a draft of a contract on Friday, so I got here early to look it over in case the author called me this morning. What are you doing here, Miss Lady?" Faith asked as she picked up four large manila envelopes from her chair. All of them were unsolicited manuscripts—she placed them on the floor by the corner of her desk, on top of a pile that reached almost knee high. She'd get to them when and if she had time. She didn't want to miss out on the next best-seller from an unknown author, but just keeping up with the manuscripts that she had requested based on query letters—one-page letters written by authors, telling an agent a little about the book and asking for permission to send a manuscript—was an overwhelming task. Sometimes the unsolicited ones stayed unread for months.

"I decided to stop over after I drove Carol to the airport. She's spending the week with her brother in Oakland." Ann gave a slight shrug of the shoulders and then slid her fingers through her pale blond hair. She was almost a dead ringer for Gwyneth Paltrow—the pale skin, the innocent-looking blue eyes, she even had the charm and poise, thanks to the finishing school her parents had sent her to as a teenager. It would be hard, though, to imagine Gwyneth laboring over piles of manuscripts in an office building in the middle of Harlem. "I didn't feel like going back to the apartment so I decided to get some work done myself."

"Aww, I know how it is. Henry left this morning for Chicago. How long will your sweetie be gone?" Faith asked sympathetically.

"A week. She wanted me to go but I told her I had too much work to do."

"Is that the brother who came to our office Christmas party last year?"

"No. This is the one that swears that he'll never set foot in Carol's apartment as long as she's involved in an immoral relationship with a woman." Ann slammed a desk drawer shut.

"Oh. That brother," Faith said weakly.

Faith and Ann had met while they were English majors at Columbia University—and on the surface, the two had nothing in common. Ann was from the Beacon Hill section of Boston and had grown up playing with the Kennedy grandkids. Her idea of relaxing was sipping a chardonnay while listening to the Broadway cast album of the musical *Cats* on her dorm room stereo. She seldom left the campus area, except to attend literary readings in Greenwich Village or concerts at Carnegie Hall when her upper-crust parents made excursions to the city to spend time with their youngest daughter. She had no friends on campus and didn't seem to want any. Her dorm mate had given up trying to form a relationship with her late in their freshman year and the buzz around campus was that she was a blue-blooded snob.

Faith and Ann shared several classes during their four years at Columbia, but they never spoke and barely nodded to each other in passing. Like Ann, Faith had no time for campus life and no desire to make friends. She'd even dropped the pals she hung around with in elementary school after the incident with Papa and Hope. She didn't want to get involved in anyone's personal life, and she certainly didn't want anyone prying into hers.

As far as Faith was concerned, she was in school for only one reason—to get her degree and get the hell out. She attended classes during the day, then rushed off to relieve Henry as cashier at the small candy store he had bought, so that he could attend his evening classes at NYU, where he majored in finance. The only exception was on the third Wednesday of every month, when the Black Student Union sponsored evening lectures by visiting professors and the so-called Black Intelligentsia.

John Henrik Clarke, a historian and a resident of Harlem, was invited to speak early in Faith's senior year. When Faith rushed in late, she was amazed and dismayed to find no empty seats in the small auditorium. Not only had the students come out to hear Clarke speak, many people in the community had as well.

After standing for twenty minutes, she noticed that a seat at the end of an aisle had a sweater thrown over the back, but no occupant.

"Excuse me, is this seat vacant?" she whispered to the young woman sitting next to it.

"No. I'm sorry, let me move my things for you," came the reply. No smile of apology or welcome crossed Ann Swanson's face, but neither was there a sign of annoyance. Ann stared straight ahead for the next forty-five minutes, seemingly engrossed in the lecture. Faith looked down at the young woman's lap to see if she had a tape recorder because it was obvious she wasn't taking notes, but there was none. Now why would this chick be sitting here if she's not taking notes for some African-American Studies class? Faith wondered. There were often a few whites at the Black Student Union lectures, but in the four years that Faith had been attending, she had never seen Ann.

"Are you studying Clarke?" Faith asked in a casual tone as she and Ann gathered up their things after the lecture had ended. She hated asking, but her curiosity had simply gotten the better of her.

"Studying?" Ann furrowed her brow.

"Are you reading his essays in a class or something?"

"No." Ann offered no explanation.

"Oh." Faith decided not to push. She headed out of the auditorium and walked to the corner of 118th Street and Amsterdam, debating whether to take the bus or catch a cab to the apartment she and Henry shared on 155th Street and Edgecomb Avenue. It was a warm night for October, and she almost decided to walk, but just then it started to rain. She held her hand out for a cab.

"Taxi," she called out to an approaching yellow cab. It was a habit she had picked up from her mother, although she realized that the drivers probably couldn't hear her voice above the noisy street sounds.

The cab stopped in front of her, and she reached over to open the passenger door, when the vehicle suddenly started moving again.

"Hey," was all she could get out as she watched the cab stop again ten feet away, in front of Ann Swanson.

Ann tapped on the driver's window and he obligingly rolled it down.

"Can you take me to Montclair, New Jersey? I'll pay double the meter and forty dollars over."

"I'm not 'sposed to go out city, lady," the driver replied in a thick accent. "Make it fifty dollars over."

"Deal." Ann looked over at Faith, who was standing at her original spot, speechless. Ann opened the passenger door and sat halfway in, her legs still on the pavement, before turning back and shouting to Faith, "Of course I know what he just did is illegal, but I'm really not willing to give up my ride. How about I drop you off where you're going?"

"What?" Faith quickly walked over.

"Ethically, I know I should just give you the cab, but I really need to get to New Jersey. Why don't I drop you off wherever you're going? You get a free ride and you get to tell the driver off while he drives," Ann said in an even tone.

"Hey, lady, what you doing?" the driver demanded, turning around to look at Ann.

"Mr. . . ." Ann looked at the cab's license posted on the bulletproof partition, "Mr. Oluwole, I'm offering my friend a ride, and before you try and pull off with me in your cab, let me inform you that my father is the head of the New York State Taxi and Limousine Commission. One telephone call from me and you'll never be able to drive a taxi in this city again."

She slid over in the seat and looked at Faith. "Are you getting in? I'm really running rather late."

"Oh yeah, I'm getting in," Faith huffed.

"I can't believe that you would pull something like that," Faith yelled at the driver after the taxi sped off. "It's bad enough with white drivers, but you're black and you would do that to a sister?"

"I'm very sorry." The driver muttered.

"That's all you have to say? That you're sorry?" Faith spat.

"And you're African, aren't you? What part of Africa are you from?"

"Nigeria," the driver mumbled.

"Where? I didn't hear you!"

"None of your business," the driver yelled as he glared at her through the rearview mirror.

"He said he's from Nigeria," Ann said to Faith calmly. She then tapped the partition behind the driver's head. "Hey, mind your manners, please."

"Oh, you're just getting a kick out of this, aren't you?" Faith turned to face Ann.

"A little. You'd better tell the cabbie where you're going, though. I think I mentioned that I'm already running late." Ann shrugged, then opened her purse and pulled out her cell phone. "I hope you'll excuse me, but I have to call Uncle Philip and wish him a happy birthday."

It wasn't until two weeks later, when she was rushing to a biology class, that Faith saw Ann again.

"Hey." She tapped Ann on the shoulder.

"Oh. Hi. How are you doing?" Ann looked surprised.

"Fine, fine. Listen, I want to apologize for my behavior the other night. I was just so pissed off at what happened that I was taking it out on everybody."

"No problem," Ann replied with a shrug.

"Well, did you make it to New Jersey in time?" Faith fumbled for something to say.

"I was an hour late. But it wasn't a big deal."

"Oh, okay. Well, listen, thanks for the ride. I can't believe I didn't even say thank you that night. But like I said, I was just so pissed off." Faith smiled and turned to walk away.

"Hey." Faith turned back to Ann, who had already started walking in the opposite direction. "What did your father do when you told him?"

Ann turned around with a puzzled look on her face. "When I told him what?"

"About the taxi driver. You did tell him, right?"

Ann broke out in the first grin Faith had seen on her face. "Oh, I was lying."

"About what?"

"Daddy doesn't head the taxi commission; he lives in Boston. I just said that to get the driver's attention." She turned and walked away, leaving Faith laughing in the hallway.

The two remained casual friends for the rest of the semester. Ann, Faith discovered, wasn't a snob. She just didn't care enough about most things or people to pay them much attention. She would ignore a millionaire just as quickly as she would ignore a panhandler on the street. And arguing simply wasn't her style. If she disagreed with someone, she would simply shrug her shoulders and walk away. But the few things she did care about, she cared about passionately— like books. Ann was drawn to novels of all different genres; exquisite writing was the only requirement. One of her favorite historical novels had been *Confessions of Nat Turner* by William Styron, which she had read at thirteen. She was browsing around a bookstore during her freshman year at Columbia when she came across another book that caught her attention: *William Styron's Nat Turner: Ten Black Writers Respond*. Scanning the back cover, she saw that the writers were essentially taking Styron to task for his Pulitzer Prize–winning book. She purchased the book just to see what they had to say, and threw out Styron's book the following morning.

"I was ashamed of myself for not realizing what these writers put forth so succinctly," she confided to Faith. "Styron's book was beautifully written, there was no question about that, and it was stated that it was historical fiction and not a true biography, but I think there has to be a limit to literary license. I thought that the black writers were upset because a white man had written about a black hero, but really they were upset because he turned a black hero into an apologist and a luster of white women. In reality, Nat Turner stated quite clearly that he did not regret his actions, and his so-called affection for his slave owner's wife was entirely fictional. Nat Turner was actually married to another slave. None of that stuff was factual. Styron made it up."

It was John Henrik Clarke who had edited the rebuttal book, and when she found out that he resided in New York City and frequently lectured in the area, she made it a point to go hear him whenever possible. "He was so wonderful. His views on race, on sexism, on everything . . . I'm just in complete agreement with him on everything."

After graduation, Faith started working as an assistant editor for a small publishing company in midtown Manhattan. It wasn't until three years later that she ran into Ann while waiting for a table at a restaurant. It turned out that Ann was working as an associate editor for a publishing house in Greenwich Village. When Faith confided that she was seriously considering venturing out on her own as a literary agent, Ann surprised her by saying she'd been thinking about doing the same thing. The two women decided to go into business together, and two years later Freeman & Swanson Associates was born. Faith prepared for their first argument when she suggested to Ann that they lease office space in Harlem to save money, but Ann simply shrugged her shoulders and said it was fine with her. That's how Ann dealt with most things in life, by simply shrugging her shoulders. That's why Ann's reaction to Carol's visit to her brother surprised Faith so much.

"Does Carol know how you feel about the visit?" Faith asked gently. Ann was the only person she knew who hated discussing her personal life with people more than her. That was likely one of the reasons the two of them got along as well as they did. But still, it bothered Faith to see Ann so visibly disturbed.

"She does." Ann shifted some papers on her desk.

"And?" Faith prompted.

"And that's her family." Ann shrugged.

"Well, is she even taking a position on this? I mean, that's her family, but you guys have been together for a year now, right? I would think—"

Riingggg.

Ann and Faith both looked at the telephone in puzzlement.

"No one knows I'm here, it's got to be for you," Ann finally said after the second ring.

"The only one who knows I'm here is Henry, and he would be calling on my private line."

"Freeman & Swanson Associates, may I help you?" Ann said as she picked up the telephone. "May I say who's calling? Hold on, please. I'll see if she's available." Ann pushed down the hold button. "It's Reva Sinclair."

"This early? On a Sunday morning!" Faith picked up the telephone on her desk. "Reva. How are you doing, honey? . . . No, I haven't had a chance to check my e-mail this weekend. . . . No, I haven't seen your cover yet. . . . Really? . . . When did you get it? . . . It's really that bad? . . . Well, of course I'll take a look at it. . . . No, I understand. . . . Okay, Reva, but remember, we don't have cover approval. . . . No, of course I want you to have the best cover possible, but I'm just reminding you that the publisher has the final decision. . . . I agree that they should have consulted you. . . . Of course what you think matters, honey. . . . I'm in full agreement. I tell you what, I'll go online and see if they e-mailed it to me also, and then I'll get back to you later tomorrow so we can discuss what we should do. . . . Well, I don't think anyone's there on a Sunday. . . . Okay, I'll try. But I really think we're going to have to wait until Monday. . . . Okay, Tuesday then, since you're going to be out of town. . . . Okay, I'll talk to you then." Faith hung up the telephone.

"She hates the cover." Ann smiled.

"She hates everything," Faith laughed, "but she's my biggest client and I want to keep her happy. And it's true that Dutton has been coming up with some really crappy covers lately. Did you see what they slapped on Richard Vaughn's book?"

"Please. Don't remind me." Ann shuddered. "So what are you going to do?"

Faith threw her pencil up in the air. "I'm going to take my business partner to brunch and worry about Dutton and Reva Sinclair tomorrow. Come on."

Ann laughed, but shook her head. "No, I'm going to head home. I need to take a nap."

"Oh come on. I've been dying to take you to Wilson's. They have the best brunch in town," Faith pleaded.

"Rain check," Ann said simply as she put on her coat.

"But Ann . . ."

"No, Faith. I'll see you tomorrow." She headed out the door.

"Wait a minute," Faith called out. "I wanted to ask if there's anything new on the Walter Frisby front. I was expecting a call from him over the weekend, but I haven't heard anything yet."

"Mmm . . . I left a message on your home voice mail. He called after you left Friday and said he'd get back to you in the next week or so."

Faith sighed. "Now we have to wait another couple of weeks? This crap doesn't make any sense."

"True, but if he decides to sign with us, all of this crap will be worth it. His last book sold five hundred thousand copies. That's more than two hundred thousand dollars in commissions," Ann reminded her partner.

"Oh, God, please let him sign with us." Faith clasped her hands in front of her and looked up at the ceiling.

Ann chuckled. "Well, I'll leave you to your prayers."

"Atheist!" Faith grinned.

"Mmm . . . and a sleepy atheist at that. I'll see you tomorrow."

"No, I'm going to take off tomorrow to take care of some personal business. I'll be back on Tuesday." Faith started gathering up some papers on her desk.

"What about Reva?"

"I'll call Dutton from home."

"All right, see you Tuesday." Ann started out the door again.

"Call me if you need to talk, Ann," Faith said gently.

"I won't and I don't. See you Tuesday."

4

It was locked. Faith stood dumbfounded in the cold vestibule for a moment. It must be stuck, she thought. Again she tried the knob of her mother's front door and even pushed her shoulder against the large, curtained windowpane, but the heavy wooden door refused to budge.

Mommy always made sure the front door was unlocked—she hated getting up to open it for people, and the brownstone wasn't equipped with a security buzzer. What the heck is going on here? Faith wondered as she fished her keys from her pocketbook.

Now if this doesn't beat all, she thought. The key wouldn't fit in the lock. Ignoring the doorbell, Faith started pounding her gloved fist against the door.

"Hold your horses! Hold your horses! Dang, I'm coming!" The door swung open to reveal Hope, holding a cigarette and a bottle of Heineken and wearing a huge smile on her face.

"Hey beautiful! What are you doing here?" she said, stepping aside so Faith could enter. "I thought you'd be at work and stuff, Baby Girl."

"I took the day off," Faith said slowly. "Where's Mom?"

"Downtown at court," Hope said lightly as they walked into their mother's living quarters. Faith wrinkled her nose with distaste at the dirty white cardigan that Hope wore over a red tube-top. Her oil-stained jeans sagged in the rear, a testament to Hope's sudden weight loss, and even the red knit cap on her head couldn't hide the fact that her hair was uncombed and unkempt. And she smelled as if she hadn't bathed in days.

"What's she doing at court?" Faith leaned against the back of the couch in disbelief as Hope plopped down in their mother's bed and released the mute button on the remote so she could listen to Bob Barker announce the latest contest on *The Price Is Right*. She grabbed a large bag of Wise potato chips that were laying open on the bed and started munching.

"Hey! I asked a question!" Faith stood in front of the television, hands on hips.

"She's getting a restraining order and stuff." Hope rolled her eyes and reached around Faith's body with the remote—this time clicking the set off.

"Against?"

"Me."

Faith grunted and took off her three-quarter-length black leather coat. She turned to throw it over the back of the sofa, but decided against it. She folded it over her arm, then walked over and sat in the armchair.

"I guess I'll wait a while for her." She leaned down and picked up an old issue of *Savoy* magazine off the floor. The cover, which featured actress Gabrielle Union, was damp and sticky from spilled orange juice, but the type on the inside pages was still legible.

"She called me a couple of times this weekend, and I promised I'd stop by today," Faith said as she looked over the table of contents.

"Hmph. I'm surprised you waited this long." Hope frowned and then stuffed a handful of potato chips in her mouth, chasing it down with a swig of Heineken.

Faith flipped through the magazine, ignoring Hope's subtle invitation for conversation. She stopped when she reached a two-page layout on Gabrielle Union. Hmm, those are some really nice shoes, she thought as she traced her fingers over the gold high-heel sandals with straps that wrapped three times around the ankle. She flipped further into the magazine until she reached the fashion credits on page 129. Two hundred and fifty dollars? she thought as she closed the magazine with a grimace. Hmph, they aren't that damn nice.

"So? You're not even going to ask for my side of the story?" Hope asked as she noisily chewed with her mouth open.

"Nope." Faith reopened the magazine and started flipping through pages again.

"Come on. Why not?"

"Because I'm not interested." Faith stopped at an article on the Clinton legacy.

"I bet Mommy told you her side," Hope pleaded.

"I wasn't interested then, either."

"Oh come on, Baby Girl. Please?"

"Hope, please." Faith sighed and put the magazine aside once more—it had proven useless as a shield against her twin. "It's not something I care to discuss. You know I try and stay out of these things."

"See, but you're playing favorites. You listened to Mommy but you won't listen to me." Hope jumped up from the bed, knocking the bag of potato chips to the floor, and knelt down in front of Faith. "Come on, Baby Girl, you've got to let me tell you what really happened."

"*No!* You're always trying to get me in the middle of this crap between you and Mommy!" Faith got up and walked to the bathroom door before realizing she still had her coat folded over her arm. She threw it on their mother's bed.

"Ooh, you know Mommy doesn't like people putting their coats on her bed." Hope stood up and playfully punched her twin on the shoulder.

Faith chuckled. "The whole house looks like it was struck by a hurricane and she could care less, but let someone throw a coat on the bed and she has a holy fit."

"She really just needs to move at this point, don't you think?" Hope asked. "I mean, I think it would be easier to move than to try and get this house clean and stuff."

"Please, Henry and I've been trying to get her to move to a nice apartment for years. We even offered to pay for it. But she keeps talking about holding on to this brownstone because it's an investment. Then she milks us for money to make repairs that never get done."

"That's your mother," Hope teased.

"Yeah, that's okay. My mother is still better than your mother." Faith stuck her tongue out and the two women started laughing.

"Faith, for real. You've got to talk to Mommy. I think she's going crazy." Hope walked over to the bed, picked up Faith's coat, and folded it neatly over the aluminum chair, then bent down and picked up the fallen bag of potato chips.

"What do you mean?"

"Well. For her to be saying the things she's saying and stuff. And then her changing the locks and going to get a restraining order and everything." Hope stopped suddenly and looked at her twin. "Can she really get a restraining order against me? I thought they only gave those out if someone was hitting you or trying to kill you and stuff."

"Don't ask me," Faith shrugged. "I thought you had to at least have the person up on charges, but maybe not."

"Now see what I mean? She's probably gonna go tell some more lies and stuff and maybe even say that I hit her or something." Hope started pacing the floor. "I'm telling you she's having a nervous breakdown and stuff. I don't know why you ain't listening."

"Because I don't want to get involved."

"Now, see, you're being all silly and stuff." Hope stopped and smiled at Faith. "You're her daughter and my twin sister. There ain't no way you couldn't be involved."

"Yeah, right." Faith grunted and sat back down.

"You gonna let me tell you what really happened?" Hope asked.

"Go ahead and tell me your side of the story," Faith answered carefully.

"Dang. Finally!" Hope walked over and sat on the side of Miss Irene's bed. "See . . . I was in my room and Ronald came in there without knocking and stuff and asked me to run to the store. I wasn't all the way dressed, but I don't know if he knew that before he came in there and stuff. Maybe he did and maybe he didn't. I don't know. I think he was kinda drunk."

"Anyway," she continued, "so I was standing up and I had my shirt on, but no pants. I mean, I had panties on and all that. But, anyway, I was just telling him to leave and I'd be out there in a minute, and Mommy comes busting in calling me a dirty little heifer and telling me to get out of her house and stuff." Hope's eyes filled with tears as she talked. "I tried to explain to her that the only reason his pants were loose was because he unbuckled his belt to tuck in his shirt, but she wouldn't listen.

"So I leave because I see how upset she is and I ain't want her blood pressure going up and stuff. And I stay away for a couple of days and then I come back this morning to see how she's doing and she's done had the lock on the front door changed. Tina had to let me in. And she told me that Mommy was going around telling people that she caught me in bed with Ronald." Tears slowly trickled down Hope's cheeks, and she had to fight back the sobs as she spoke. "I don't know why she be doing this stuff to me."

Tears instinctively welled up in Faith's eyes as she watched Hope cover her face with her hands and start rocking back and forth as if in physical pain. Faith chewed her lip as she fought back a strong instinct to take Hope in her arms and comfort her. There was something about Hope that brought out a protective instinct in people—she was always so sweet and kind that everyone wanted to make sure the friendly smile she kept on her face never disappeared.

Once, when they were in second grade at PS 136, Hope cut in on the lunch line and a little boy with uncombed hair and a runny nose pulled her ponytail in retaliation. When she tried to get away, he grabbed hold of her brand-new sailor's suit dress, ripping the sleeve. The little boy was new to the school and didn't know the penalty for making Hope cry. He soon found out. Seven boys from the second and third grades waited for him in the schoolyard after classes were dismissed and beat the poor kid so bad that he peed on himself. Pee-Pee Bobby was the designated punching bag for the rest of the year. His mother wisely transferred him to another school the following September. As for Hope, she was given an extra serving of ice cream by the school lunchroom workers to calm her down, and her teacher used her own money to buy a brand new dress on 125th Street.

It wasn't that Hope demanded, or even expected, to get that kind of treatment—she just got it. Even when Hope was bad and caused her little mischief, people—especially Faith—always made excuses for her behavior. But now, nausea flooded Faith as she listened to Hope make her own excuses.

"Look, I think I'm going to go ahead and split," Faith said finally.

"Dang. You're just going to leave and stuff?" Hope's mouth gaped as she looked up at her sister. "You ain't even gonna say something about what I just said?"

Hope slowly rose from the bed and walked over to the bedroom window without looking at Faith. She stared outside at the concrete backyard for a moment before speaking again.

"It ain't fair that Mommy's always picking on me and calling me all kinds of sluts and stuff and she don't never bother you." Hope crossed her arms over her chest. "You know she was accusing me of going with grown men when I was just a kid. And I swear I was a virgin until I was sixteen."

"Hope, you had your first abortion at fourteen," Faith said quietly.

"Okay, that's true . . ." Hope was unfazed, "but that was a slipup. I mean, dang. It ain't like I was one of those girls running 'round wild, jumping from bed to bed like Mommy always be making me out to be."

"Come on, Hope, you were slipping out of our bedroom window, meeting the guy from the record store one night, the guy who ran the laundromat the next, and the guy who worked in the candy store the day after that—and you were only fifteen," Faith replied.

"Well, yeah, okay. So I screwed up a couple of times when I was young, but that doesn't mean Mommy should be thinking I'm screwing her man." Hope swung around to face her sister, her arms outstretched as if begging for help. "I mean, what kind of woman does she think I am?"

"You know what kind of woman she thinks you are, and you know why she thinks it, Hope. Be fair," Faith said in a reasonable tone.

"What do you mean?"

"Hope, this is me you're talking to. *Me.*" Faith let out a big sigh and walked across the room away from Hope. "Why are you standing there trying to convince me you didn't do things that I know damn well you've done? Save that nonsense for the police, or the DA, or the priest—whomever—but why would you even think you could come out of your face with that innocent act to me?"

The twins stood in silence, facing away from each other. Faith sighed again and turned to look at Hope, still standing by the window.

"You know," she said slowly, "all of this is really Papa's fault. If he hadn't—"

"Oh, please don't start that shit again!" Hope continued to stare out of the dirty window.

"Well, it is, Hope! It's because of him that you do so many messed-up things! Don't you even understand what he did to you?" Faith tried to keep her voice level, but her blood boiled as it did every time she thought about Papa. Why is it, she wondered, that no one wants to admit the evil he had done to the entire family?

"He ain't do nothing to me!" Hope snapped. "I don't want to talk about it anymore. You just hate him and stuff."

"Damn right I hate him. And you would, too, if you had any sense," Faith hissed.

"This ain't about Papa and what you think he did to me." Hope turned around and faced her sister, though she stayed by the window. "This is about Mommy always accusing me of stuff I ain't do. She's always picking on me! And you know it!"

Faith walked over and picked her coat up from the aluminum chair, brushing it off before she put it on. "Look, I really have to go."

"Look at you, overreacting and stuff," Hope whined.

"Oh please, I'm not even overreacting," Faith snapped. "I get a telephone call in the middle of the night from my mother saying that she caught my sister screwing her boyfriend. Then I come over here to find the locks changed and Mommy downtown getting a restraining order on you while you're up in her house drinking beer and watching television.

"Then I tell you, over and over and over again, that I really don't want to hear about any of this bullshit, but you insist—you plead—that I hear you out. And then I finally agree—I very reluctantly agree—and you try and hand me a whole bunch of bullshit. But what do I do? I don't get angry. I don't yell. I don't do anything but say I'm leaving, and you're saying I'm overreacting. Please."

Faith opened the bedroom door to leave, but paused with her hand still on the knob and turned to look at her sister.

"And you'd better get out of here, too, before Mommy comes home. I don't want her calling me in the middle of the night to bury a dead body."

Hope shrugged her shoulders. "Can I stay over your house for a couple of days until Mommy cools out?"

Faith winced as she imagined Henry's reaction to the request. She suddenly tilted her head and stared at her sister through slit eyes.

"Hey, where've you been staying the last couple of days, anyway?"

"At Mrs. Trumble's," Hope said with a nonchalant shrug.

"Hmph. Yeah, right."

"Huh? What do you mean?"

"I mean you've been holed up in that crack house for the last two days," Faith snapped.

"That's a lie!" Hope balled her fists and walked purposely over to Faith as if to throw a punch. I know she hasn't lost that many brain cells, Faith thought.

"Who told you that lie?" Hope demanded.

"First off, we both know it's not a lie. I give you credit, you seem to be able to hide your habit from most people, but don't deny what we both know. And second, it doesn't matter who told me." Faith looked her sister straight in the eye as she answered.

"Well, maybe I do a couple of caps now and then and stuff, but it ain't like I'm a crackhead!" Hope's face was twisted in anger and for a moment Faith thought she might actually take a swing, but she suddenly backed away with a smirk on her face.

"Yeah, I bet it was that dope-pusher boyfriend of yours that said that shit, huh?" Hope asked, tauntingly.

The verbal slap caught Faith by surprise. "Excuse me?" was all she could say.

"You heard me. I said it was probably Mr. Henry 'Cocaine' Prince that told you that lie," Hope said, backing further away, conveniently out of arm's reach.

"You know what? You're a little witch." Faith's lip curled as she spoke in a low voice. "Henry is an investment banker at one of the most prestigious brokerage firms in the country. He pulls in more than a hundred thousand a year and he doesn't have anything to do with drugs and you know it."

"Yeah, now he doesn't. But the only way he was able to pay for you and him to go to college so y'all could get fancy jobs was because he was pushing weight."

"Yeah, and so what? My man did what he had to do. *And so what?* He ain't doing it no more," Faith shouted as she advanced on her still retreating sister. "And at least he didn't have me out there selling pussy in Queens."

Hope's head jerked back as if she'd been struck, and Faith couldn't resist going for the jugular. "Yeah, I heard you're only charging five bucks for blow jobs these days! What happened? The economy's gone bad?"

"Fuck you!" Hope reared up.

"Yeah, go ahead and jump so I can have an excuse to kick your sorry little ass," Faith sneered, balling up her fists.

The room suddenly became silent as the two sisters stared threateningly at each other. Hope finally heaved a sigh and backed away.

"Little ass, huh?" she said with a weak smile. "My booty is bigger than yours."

"Uh uh, you're not joking your way out of this fight." Faith jabbed her finger in her sister's face. "If you and Mommy want to go around tearing each other up, fine. That's between y'all. But don't you *ever* try and get in my face about Henry, you hear?"

"You better get your finger outta my face," Hope said backing away again.

"You so bad, you move it," Faith snarled. "After all Henry's done for you, you're going to go attack him? You've got a lot of shit with you, you know that?"

"He ain't never done nothing for me!"

"Uh huh, that's why he beat up that pimp on Queens Boulevard when he went upside your head a couple of months ago."

"He ain't do that for me. He only got out there like that because you was up in that dude's face and he ain't want you to get hurt and stuff."

"But I wouldn't been up there in that jerk's face if it wasn't for you! And the bottom line is he wouldn't been up there defending me if I weren't up there defending you so you could go sell pussy without someone wanting to kick your ass!"

"You make me sick!" Hope shouted, and then retreated to the window.

"You make me sicker!"

Faith stood in the middle of the room—the victor.

"I'm going. See you later," she said slowly as the adrenaline eased from her blood.

"Yeah, okay," Hope said glumly from the corner. "So can I stay over your house for a couple of days and stuff?"

"Yeah, you know you can." Faith sucked her teeth. "We're proba-

bly not going to be in until late, so use your key if we're not there."
As she turned to go, she heard someone fumbling with the lock on
the outside door. "Oh shoot, Hope. You're in trouble now. Mommy's
getting ready to come in."

"Shit! I gotta get outta here." Hope shot up from the bed, knocking over the half-empty bottle of beer as she frantically ran for the
door.

"She's going to see you if you go out that way." Faith pulled her
sister back.

"Yeah, yeah . . . what should I do?" Hope's eyes were wide as she
searched for an escape. The twins heard the front door finally open
and their mother's slow, heavy footsteps coming down the hallway.

"Baby Girl, you're going to have to . . ." Faith turned around just
in time to see her sister climbing out the bedroom window.

5

Hey, sweetie . . . how did you get in here?" Miss Irene leaned on the doorjamb to catch her breath. Her face was so red from the cold air that her light-brown freckles were almost indiscernible. She reached up and poked at her glasses, which had been hanging precariously on her nose, and flashed a weak smile at her daughter.

"Would you believe the cab had to let me out on Adam Clayton Boulevard because of street construction? I had to walk all the way down the block with my bad back. And it's freezing out there."

"Mommy, look at you. Your coat is open, that's why you're freezing." Faith kissed her mother on the cheek and then helped her slip out of her black wool overcoat. She then slid the silky, navy blue scarf from her mother's neck, revealing the push-up bra cleavage of which Miss Irene was so proud, and the stylish, royal blue dress ordered from the Roman's catalogue just a week before. Her mother poked fun at large women who insisted on wearing tent dresses to try and cover up their weight. All of her mother's dresses had plunging necklines and were fitted at her forty-nine-inch waist. She actually had an hourglass figure since her bust was an impressive sixty-eight inches and her hips were seventy-three. And as much as her mother complained about her back, when she was outside she always held her head high and her shoulders straight. Miss Irene was an impressive woman.

Faith involuntarily pulled her face away when her mother's hand accidentally brushed against her face. "Mom, your hands are freezing. Why aren't you wearing your gloves?"

"I couldn't find them and I was running late," Miss Irene answered wearily. "I didn't even get a chance to put on foundation, just some moisturizer and some eye shadow. Do my lips look chapped?"

"No, you look fine. I like that shade of lipstick on you, by the way." Faith put her mother's arm over her shoulder to lend the woman support, then led her toward the bedroom.

"Cocoa Brown. I'll get you a tube next time I send someone to the drugstore."

"Just for that, I'll make you a nice cup of tea while you rest up a bit." Faith smiled and then kissed her mother on the cheek again. "But the lipstick won't look half as good on me as it does on you."

"I keep telling you to use a lip liner."

"You didn't have time to find your gloves, but you had time to put on lip liner?" Faith feigned a look of surprise.

"Priorities, sweetie. You know I'm not going to step out of this house unless I'm looking good." Miss Irene smiled, revealing the deep dimples that she had passed on to Hope, but not to Faith. She sighed deeply as they reached the bed, and then she sank down into the soft mattress.

"Make sure you put Sweet'n Low in my tea, sweetie. I'm starting my diet today. And make sure you . . ." A puzzled look crossed her face and she began to make sniffing sounds, looking around the cluttered room. "Is that beer I smell? Who was in here drinking beer?"

"Hope." Faith bent down and unzipped her mother's brown leather boot and tugged it off her foot.

"You let that heifer in my house!" Miss Irene reared back on the bed.

"Nope. She let *me* in." Faith tugged the other boot so hard, she fell over backward when it came off and almost landed in a puddle of beer that had spilled out of the bottle Hope had knocked over just minutes before.

"How did she get in here? I had the locks changed!"

"Tina let her in." Faith picked up the bottle, stood up, and slid off her own coat, throwing it over the back of the couch. "Hold on, let me get the mop."

"I'm going to kill that Tina. She knew I didn't want Hope in this house. She just did that to be cute, the old spiteful heifer," Miss Irene's voice rang out behind her. "You know what, I'm going to evict her next time she's late with her rent."

"Then who would you use as your messenger pigeon?" Faith teased as she mopped up the beer.

"What do you mean?"

"Well, we both know you didn't go downtown to get a restraining order on Hope, and we both know that you told Tina you did because you knew she would tell Hope." Faith leaned on the mop and smiled at her mother.

"What makes you think I wasn't downtown?"

"Because you would have taken someone with you to run around the different offices in the court building, getting all the paperwork for you while you sat in the lobby and drank a cup of coffee." Faith chuckled, remembering the many times she had played the role of City Hall gopher when her mother had to go to Landlord and Tenant Court to evict one of her boarders.

"Well, I would have gone if there was someone to come with me." Miss Irene fixed her mouth into a pretty pout.

"But there wasn't, so you didn't."

"Okay, I went to meet your Aunt Gloria for breakfast. Stop acting so smug," Miss Irene snapped. "And I suppose you shared the results of your analytical skills with your sister?"

"Nope. That's between you and her." Faith shrugged. "You know I don't get involved in your battles."

"Yes you do. You always take her side," Miss Irene said with a recomposed pout. "The two of you are always ganging up on me."

"Mommy, please. The only time I step in is when it looks like one of you is going to kill the other. Which, I might add, is happening pretty often lately." Faith replaced the mop in the bathroom and headed to the kitchen. "I'll have your tea ready in a moment."

"So, how's your business doing?" Miss Irene deftly sliced into the porterhouse steak and smiled at Faith in satisfaction when the dark red juices seeped onto her plate, verifying that the meat had been prepared just the way she liked. The large plate that Faith had placed on the small TV dinner stand also featured a fluffy mound of yellow rice and simmered chopped broccoli—both topped with pan drippings from the broiled steak.

Faith watched as her mother speared a small slice of steak with her fork and brought it up to her mouth, then closed her eyes in pure bliss as she chewed, not even noticing the small bit of steak juice that dripped onto her house dress. One thing about Mommy, Faith thought as she basked in the recognition of her culinary skills, she sure appreciates good cooking.

"Everything's going great, I guess, but I'm on pins and needles waiting to find out what Walter Frisby's going to do." Faith lay across the armchair, her legs dangling over the side of one torn arm, her head propped up on the other. "Man, oh man, if he signs with me, I'll have it made."

"What are your chances?"

Miss Irene's eyes never left her plate as she spoke. It was a habit that many people found annoying, thinking that she wasn't really paying attention to the conversation, but Faith knew differently.

"Sometimes I think I have an excellent shot because after all, he did approach me. Other times I think my chances are just fifty-fifty because I know it has to be hard to leave an agency that you've dealt with for the past eighteen years. Especially a prestigious agency like William Morris." Faith sighed. "But it's not like he's really taking a chance by going with me. I've been in business for three years now and everyone in the publishing world knows that I'm an excellent agent."

Miss Irene chuckled. "You know, no one would ever be able to accuse you of false modesty."

Faith shrugged. "Anyway, he said he would let me know by the end of the month. I just have to be patient, I guess." It might not hurt to invite him out to dinner, Faith suddenly thought. And Henry could probably manage to get some front-row tickets to the big boxing match at Madison Square Garden next week.

"And tell me again, why is he thinking about signing with you?" Miss Irene asked.

"Because he wants to help other 'black folks' now that he's made it big."

"And he considers you 'other black folks'? Interesting."

Faith glanced at her watch and considered whether she should let the remark pass. Only 3:00 P.M., she had some time to spare.

"So what are you saying, Mommy? That I'm not black enough?"

"No, I'm not saying that. But I know you're probably clearing a profit of six figures every year . . ."

Faith smiled inwardly as Miss Irene glanced in her direction to gauge whether she was in the right ballpark—her mother had been trying to figure out Faith's income for years. Faith kept her face expressionless and her mother continued on.

" . . . and I know Henry's bringing in six figures. So when I think about someone reaching back to help other blacks, I just think they would want to help someone who needs more help. If I were looking to give a handout, you two wouldn't necessarily come to mind." Miss Irene smiled and looked up from her plate, gleefully anticipating the debate she had set in motion.

Faith smiled back. This one was going to be good—class issues always made for passionate discussion. But the telephone perched on her mother's bed rang before she could form a response.

Miss Irene glanced at the telephone in annoyance, but pushed her dinner tray out of the way and picked up the receiver.

"Hello? . . . Oh, hi, sweetie. . . . I'm doing well. What about yourself? . . . That's good to hear. And Carol? . . . Oh that's wonderful."

Faith frowned, then fished inside her pocketbook for her cell phone. Why would Ann be calling her at her mother's house instead of on the cell? The cell phone was on and the message light wasn't flashing to indicate she had missed any calls.

"Oh, you're kidding? . . . That's just wonderful! I'm so happy for the two of you. . . . No, Hope didn't mention it to me at all. The little heifer. . . . Of course I'm coming! . . . June what? What day of the week is that? . . . A Sunday wedding, oh that is so nice. . . . Where's it going to be held? . . . St. Martin's? Here in Harlem? . . . Oh, you have a St. Martin's on Long Island. I didn't think you were going to get married on 122nd Street. . . . Well, please send me an invitation. You are going to mail out invitations, aren't you? . . . Okay . . . I'm just checking. Some brides these days think if they invite you by telephone, they don't have to send out invitations. Oh, and is it okay

if I bring a guest? . . . Okay, sweetie. . . . Thank you so much for inviting me. . . . I'm sorry, what did you say? . . . Oh! Faith doesn't
know? . . . You want to surprise her. . . . Well, sure. . I won't say a
word. . . . Okay, sweetie. . . . Thanks again. . . . You take care now."

Faith's mouth gaped as her mother hung up the telephone. "Ann
and Carol are getting married? You're kidding."

"Well, you're not supposed to know. She wants to surprise you."

"Why does she want to surprise me?"

"She didn't say, and I didn't ask." Miss Irene shrugged. "I feel bad
enough already that I let you in on the wedding, but she should have
told me she didn't want you to know before she started talking. I
would have kept the secret. She said she called over here the other
day and told Hope, though. The little witch never even mentioned
she called. That sister of yours is just garbage, Faith."

"So, Ann and Carol are getting married. Deep. I wonder why
they don't want me to know." Faith said out loud to herself. "What
could that little vixen have up her sleeve?"

"So . . . I have a question." Miss Irene was once again enjoying
her meal. "Is one a bride and one a groom? Or are they both brides?"

Faith tilted her head sideways as she contemplated the question.
"You know, that's a good one." She thought about it for another
minute.

"I'd guess they'd both be brides," she said slowly.

"Really? So they're both going to walk down the aisle wearing
fancy wedding dresses?" Miss Irene asked as she chewed happily.
"That should be interesting. I've got to remember to bring a camera."

Faith shrugged. It wasn't like she could ask her resident lesbian
expert about the protocol, because Ann didn't even want her to
know.

What the hell is that all about? she wondered again. It couldn't be
that I offended her, because then she wouldn't want my family there

either. And Ann would tell me if she were mad at me, wouldn't she?

Faith watched her mother finish off her plate of food, then push the tray back with a sigh of satisfaction. Miss Irene then lay across the bed with her eyes closed, as if basking in an afterglow.

Maybe I should call the house when I know Ann isn't there and just start some idle chatter with Carol? Maybe she'll explain what's going on, Faith thought. But no, that won't work. Ann and Carol live in the same apartment, but have separate phones—darn them. And there's no reason for me to call Carol's phone to talk to Ann. Shoot.

"So, what do you think Hope's going to do now that I've kicked her little ass out on the street?"

Miss Irene's sharp words snapped Faith back to reality. It wasn't like her mother to curse, and the words seemed to come out of nowhere.

"What do you mean?" she stammered.

"I'm not letting her stay here, and Mrs. Trumble is finally in the hospital, so she can't stay with her, and I made sure Aunt Gloria knows better than to take her in," Miss Irene said with a satisfied smirk. "I don't know where she's been staying for the last couple of days, but she's going to wear out her welcome eventually."

"Yeah, I guess so." Faith looked at her. She got up from the chair and reached for her coat, which was lying over the back of the couch. "God, look at the time. I've got to split, Mommy. I'll give you a call tomorrow."

"I thought you were going to spend the day with me." Miss Irene said in a disappointed voice.

"I've already spent the whole morning here, and most of the afternoon. I need to stop by my office before I go home, and I'm trying to get home kind of early for a change. Henry has to go out of town again tomorrow and I want to fix him something special this evening," Faith said. She leaned over and gave her mother a quick peck on the cheek.

"I promise I'll come over and cook dinner this weekend. Whatever you want, okay? Just send Tina or someone to the store to buy the groceries."

"Smothered chicken?" her mother asked hopefully.

"I thought you were going on a diet," Faith teased. "You had steak today and you want smothered chicken in a couple of days, what kind of diet is that?"

"I know what I'm doing," Miss Irene said indignantly. "As big as I am, I can't be going on a starvation diet. I have to ease into it. I'm probably not going to eat another thing today."

"Mom, you already had a giant-sized breakfast and lunch."

"Look, are you going to cook me my smothered chicken or what?" Miss Irene asked irritably.

Faith laughed. "Smothered chicken, greens, red rice, and biscuits. How's that?"

"Sounds delicious." Miss Irene grinned. "And pick up some coconut cake from that bakery up your way. Ooh, and stop and get some Breyers vanilla ice cream."

"Sounds like a plan. I'll be over around five." Faith gathered up the dishes to place in the kitchen sink on her way out the door. "Okay, Mommy, I'll see you this weekend. Love you."

"Love you, too, sweetie."

Faith was almost to the front door when she heard her mother's voice ring out.

"Faith . . . wait!"

She walked back through the kitchen and into her mother's room. "What's wrong?"

"I have to give you the new keys." Miss Irene dangled a small key ring in front of her.

"Oh, I forgot." Faith reached out for the keys, and her mother's hand closed tightly around hers.

"Where's Hope staying tonight?" She demanded.

"We'll talk about that when I come over tomorrow." Faith quickly squeezed her hand and took the keys from her mother's grasp.

"Get back over here," Miss Irene shouted as Faith made a beeline for the door. "You better not be letting that little heifer stay over at your house!"

"I'll call you later, Mommy. Love you!" Faith said as she reached the hallway. She could hear her mother calling out to her even as she opened the front door to leave.

"Faith get back in here! I'm not playing with you!"

Faith escaped into the cold air and started briskly walking to the corner to hail a cab. Mental note: Take the telephone off the hook and don't answer the cell phone, she said to herself. Mommy's going to be on the warpath.

6

To cab or not to cab, that was the question facing Faith as she walked toward Seventh Avenue after fleeing her mother's house. It would take two buses and a good thirty-five minutes to get from 119th and Lenox Avenue, where Miss Irene lived, to the apartment Faith shared with Henry on 155th Street and Edgecomb Avenue, and she would still wind up having to walk three blocks. Taking a cab would get her there a lot faster and cost about five dollars—quick and affordable. She stepped off the sidewalk and waved her right arm to hail a taxi—not even noticing if there was one in sight. An unmarked car stopped in front of her, prompting Faith to peer in at the driver instead of getting in. No partition, no meter, no livery license posted on the dashboard, she noticed.

"Where ya going?" the grizzly looking driver growled at her through the half-open window.

"One fifty-fifth and Edgecomb," Faith answered.

"Seven dollars. Hop in, babe." The driver faced straight ahead, put the car in gear, then gunned the engine.

Faith stepped back from the car and chuckled. The guy was unlicensed, uncouth—and he was overcharging. "No, that's okay. I'll get another cab."

"What's wrong?" The driver leaned back toward the window. "Okay, I'll make it six dollars."

"Thanks, but I'll pass." Faith started walking away from the car.

"Fucking bitch!" the driver yelled before peeling out.

"Asshole!" Faith shouted back at the fleeing car, then turned to see if anyone had noticed her futile profanity. This was New York; no one noticed. She pulled the collar of her coat closer around her neck and took her leather gloves out of her pocketbook. It was cold, but it wasn't freezing, and she was dressed warmly. Might as well just make the forty-block walk, she thought. She needed time to figure out how she was going to explain to Henry that Hope would be staying with them, anyway. Those two had never really gotten along.

"Faith? Is that you, Faith?"

Faith turned around to see an elderly woman in a wheelchair being pushed by a younger woman who looked to be about twenty.

"Hi, Mrs. Shelling." Faith walked over and kissed the woman's wizened cheek. "I haven't seen you in forever."

"That's because you don't come around to see an old woman anymore." Mrs. Shelling flashed her badly fitting dentures.

"I'm sorry, it's just that . . ." Faith began.

"Oh, shut up. I'm joshing you, girl," Mrs. Shelling interrupted. "I know you're a career girl. I was a carrier girl, too, you know." She turned in her chair to address the girl. "Stop fidgeting with my chair, Rhonda. I'm trying to talk."

The girl rolled her eyes in response.

"My home health aide," Mrs. Shelling explained as she turned back to Faith. "She's on the clock for another two hours, but she's trying to get me home so she can sneak out early again."

Faith smiled to suppress a giggle as Rhonda loudly sucked her teeth. Mrs. Shelling was a retired nurse, and a woman who in her younger days didn't take any stuff from anyone, and her attitude hadn't changed with her age.

"Anyway, I wanted to thank you for the books you've been sending me. Gives me something to do while I'm stuck in this chair with my bad hip. I really enjoyed the book about black medical pioneers that Hope brought over last week."

"Oh, sure. My pleasure," Faith answered, trying not to reveal the surprise in her voice. She hadn't sent any books to Mrs. Shelling in months. But she did remember the book. Hope had visited her office a few weeks before and asked for the copy when she saw it on one of the bookshelves.

"How is Hope, anyway? I haven't seen her in a few days," Mrs. Shelling continued. "She usually stops in and makes me a cup of tea in the mornings."

"She's okay. She's just been keeping a low profile lately," Faith answered politely. "I'll tell her you asked for her."

"Please do. That sister of yours is a gem. I told her she should get a job as a home health aide since she seems to like taking care of people. She may as well get paid for it."

"You ready yet? It's cold out here," Rhonda grumbled.

"Be quiet, child. The cold air is good for you," Mrs. Shelling snapped.

"Well, I gots to get you home so you can take your medicine." Rhonda poked her lips out.

"Oh, now all of a sudden you care whether I get my medicine in time." Mrs. Shelling gave a little laugh, then addressed Faith again. "I'm going to let you go ahead wherever it is you're going, Faith. But make sure you tell Hope to stop over and see me again soon. It's nice to have someone around who actually cares if you live or die."

"I'll tell her." Faith leaned over and kissed the woman again.

"All right, you can take me home now," Mrs. Shelling said over her shoulder to Rhonda. "And don't think I didn't know you were behind me rolling your eyes all this time."

Faith shook her head as she started back on her way. Hope was something else. She never ever mentioned her visits to Mrs. Shelling, or that she was telling the woman the books she was bringing were gifts from Faith.

Screeeeeeeeeech!

"Stupid ho! You don't see you ain't got the goddamned light?"

Faith jumped back on the curb, her heart beating wildly. The gypsy cab had so come close to hitting her that two men, both of whom had been standing in front of the corner restaurant, came running to see if she was all right.

"Fucking downtown bitch!" The cabbie spat out his window and the stream of spittle barely missed her.

"Hey, hey! What the fuck's the matter with you, asshole? You ain't gotta be cussing at the woman and spitting and shit!" A man with a black skullcap grabbed her arm and pulled her back as he shouted at the driver.

"That bitch must be drunk. She walked right out in front of my cab, man!" the cabbie screamed back in explanation.

"I don't give a shit. Don't be cussing at one of our queens like that, you pussy motherfucker. Drive the fuck on off before me and this god here kick your stink ass," the skullcapped man yelled back.

The driver muttered something inaudible, then sped off through the red light, almost hitting another pedestrian in his hurry to get away.

Faith looked up at the man whose arm still protectively encircled her shoulders. He looked familiar.

"You okay, Queen?" he asked when he finally stopped cursing in the direction of the fleeing taxi.

"Yeah, I'm okay . . . thanks." Hmm, Queen? she thought as she took a good look at the man. Something about him was familiar, and his addressing her as "Queen" helped her place him—not his name—but at least she knew where they must have met. He was in the organization that Henry belonged to as a teenager, the Five Percenters. A kind of offshoot of the Nation of Islam, the group was popular in New York in the seventies and still had a small but loyal following. They referred to every man as "God," and every woman as "Queen," but there didn't seem to be any rule in their religion about using foul language, as the man had just proven.

"You sure you okay?" the man asked again. "You look pretty shaken."

"No, no . . . I'm fine." Faith managed a weak smile of reassurance and gratitude. "Thanks for standing up for me like that."

"That's what I'm supposed to do, Queen. I can't have that nigger disrespecting God Raheem's queen like that."

"No, really . . . I'm fine." Faith managed a weak laugh. It had been years since someone had referred to Henry as Raheem. "I've always had bad luck with taxi cabs. Even when I'm not riding in them."

"You want me to walk you to your destination, Queen?"

"No, I've got a way to go and I don't want to take up your time. Thanks, though."

"Okay, well you tell God Raheem that God Shafik was looking out for his queen."

"I will." Faith started to put her hand out to shake Shafik's hand, but changed her mind and hugged him instead. "Thank you so much, God. I'll let Raheem know you're still out here holding it down."

"Yeah, do that," Shafik answered gruffly. "And tell him not to make himself a stranger."

"And Queen!" Shafik yelled out as Faith walked away. "I know you don't remember me, but I was with Raheem when he found you that night."

Faith paused, then walked back over to Shafik, who stood in the middle of the sidewalk with his arms crossed, smiling at her with a look of obvious pride. "I remember, God," she said gently. "And thank you."

Faith was fifteen when she ran away from home for the third time, after Papa had tried to reach into her blouse and squeeze her budding breasts, as he had tried so many times before. When she bit him on the arm, he laughed and let her go, telling her that she was a whore and he was going to "get that pussy" one way or the other. Her response was to run upstairs to the second-floor bathroom and grab a razor blade that she carefully hid in the palm of her hand. He grabbed at her again when she went back downstairs, just as she knew he would. Instead of biting, though, she slashed at his arm with the razor, slicing him on the forearm. He pulled back in surprise, and she lunged at him, trying to slice his throat, but he put his hand up just in time and she sliced through the artery on his wrist instead. He started yelling as blood spurted out, covering the two of them. She lunged at him again, but he backhanded her across the mouth and knocked her backward with his good arm while yelling for her mother. When Miss Irene made it down the stairs, she didn't even ask what had happened, but she probably didn't need to. Faith was crying while holding a bloody razor, and Papa was holding his wrist to try and stop the squirting blood while calling Faith a bunch of whores. Miss Irene ran to Papa and yelled for Faith to stop crying and call an ambulance before Papa bled to death. When Faith refused, the frightened woman wrapped a towel around Papa's wrist, pulled him into the street, and hailed a taxi to take them to the hospital.

Faith waited by the telephone praying for the worst, but her prayers went unanswered. Her mother called from the hospital to say that Papa would be okay. She actually acted as if she was giving Faith good news. Faith didn't even bother to pack a bag. She stayed at different friends' houses at first, but after a week her welcome had worn out with all of them. Determined not to return home, she made a bed of old rags and drifted off into an uneasy sleep on the roof of a South Bronx tenement around midnight.

She awakened a few hours later when she heard a voice ask in a hushed, but worried voice, "Is she breathing?"

A wave of fear rushed through Faith's body. She'd heard the horror stories about girls who were gang-raped and thrown off of roofs. And from the murmuring going on around her, she knew there were at least three men, maybe more. There would be no way she could jump up and run fast enough to escape them. Maybe if she just lay really still, they would think she was dead and go about their business.

"I don't know. You think we should shake her or something?"

She managed to stifle a scream as someone landed a sharp kick to the middle of her back.

"Shit, Jerry, if she wasn't dead, she is now. Why you gonna do something stupid like that?"

"I was checking to see if she alive, man," a deep voice answered.

Faith felt the warmth of a hand on her cheek. She squinted her eyes to see if she could see who was touching her. Suddenly she felt a sharp pain on the back of her head. This time she couldn't hold back the scream as she scrambled to her knees.

"Jerry, man, what the hell is wrong with you? Why you gotta go kick her in the head like that?" The teenager who had been crouching over Faith jumped to his feet to confront the man behind her.

"Chill, motherfucker," Jerry said threateningly.

"Come on, now, you gods cool out," a third man said soothingly.

"Yo, Shafik, you tell him to cool the fuck out before I kick his young little punk ass," Jerry growled. "And I ain't no fucking god. I'm a man, motherfucker."

"You okay?" The teenager knelt down and placed a hand on Faith's shoulder.

"Yeah," Faith mumbled as she tried to scramble to her feet. The pain from the blow to her back made her fall to her knees again.

"Here, let me help you." The teenager threw Faith's arm over his shoulder and hoisted her to her feet, but she backed away from him as soon as she was standing. That's when she noticed there were six men, all of whom looked to be in their mid to late twenties, except for the teenager who had spoken to her. They stood staring at her, and that's when she noticed that her blouse was partially open, revealing her bare breasts. She tried to fasten it, but realized with dismay that the top three buttons were missing. She'd probably popped them when she tried to get up. The teenager noticed her agitation and quickly pulled off his light V neck sweater, revealing a hairless and chiseled chest. He held the sweater out to Faith, but she simply backed away, crossing her hands over her chest to try and hide her body.

"What are you doing up here?" the teenager asked gently.

"I'm waiting for my father. He had to go to the store, but he'll be right back," Faith said quickly.

"He left you here by yourself? What kind of shit is that?" the man called Shafik asked.

"He said he'd be right back. I think I'll just go and see what's taking him so long." Faith tried to back away toward the door and make it inside the building and down the stairs, but Jerry, the man who had kicked her, blocked her path.

"Naw, if he said for you to wait for him up here, just wait for him." He grabbed her arm and roughly pulled her away from the door. "You cats can leave, I'll wait with her and make sure she's okay."

"Jerry, man, if she said she wants to leave, let her leave," the teenager said in a measured tone.

"Punk! Didn't I already tell you to back the fuck up? You fucking Five Percenters are always talking about protecting women and shit and then you gonna let this girl go out in the street this time of night by herself? What kind of shit is that? I'm going to stay up here and wait with her for her old man, okay? Now back the fuck off."

"I'll walk her downstairs, then." The teenager reached his hand out, and Faith tried to grab it, but Jerry yanked her away, never loosening his tight grip on her arm.

"You don't trust me, motherfucker? I said I can handle this. Now why don't you guys just go ahead and split?"

"Jerry, what the fuck's wrong with you, man?" Shafik walked over and stood next to the teenager. "Why don't you just let her go and let's smoke this joint like we came up here to do?"

"'Cause I feel like doing something else!" Faith was struggling to free herself as the men argued, but Jerry's grip only tightened.

"Man, she ain't nothing but a little girl," Shafik reasoned.

"Man, shut the fuck up and move the fuck out. I ain't gonna do nothing but make sure she's okay," Jerry yelled. "What? You wanna try me motherfucker?"

"Man, we ain't come up here to fight . . ." Shafik tried to reason with Jerry.

"Fuck that!" the teenager suddenly shouted as he pushed past Shafik and advanced toward Jerry. "Let her go or I'll kick your funky ass right up and right now."

Jerry laughed and shoved Faith toward the three men who were standing behind him. One of them grabbed her, pinning her arms together behind her back as she screamed and struggled to break free. One of the men scurried over to the roof door and into the building, obviously wanting no part in what was about to happen.

"Oh, youngblood wants to try me, huh?" Jerry threw up his hands and assumed a boxing stance. "Okay, motherfucker, let's see what you got."

"I got your back, God," Shafik cried out as the two men circled each other as if in a boxing ring. "This is a fair one, y'all. I'll cut the first motherfucker that tries to jump in this shit."

Jerry's arm darted out and landed a solid blow to the side of the teenager's head. It was the only punch the man landed. His young foe danced away, then darted back in quickly, delivering two jabs to Jerry's right jaw, then followed with a left uppercut to his chin. Jerry stumbled back, but the teenager followed him, delivering a series of haymakers to the man's face. Jerry was now against the door, trying to cover up his face as the furious teen threw punch after punch at his head and kidneys.

One of Jerry's friends jumped behind the boy, punching him in the back of the head, but the teenager didn't seem to notice.

"Back the fuck off!"

Faith screamed as she saw Shafik, knife in hand, approach the man who had interfered in the fight. But before Shafik could reach him, the teenager swung around and kicked the man in the groin. The man doubled over and fell to his knees, and the boy turned back around and started kicking Jerry, who lay on the ground in a fetal position.

"Now, let her go," Shafik said as he approached the man who was still holding Faith.

"Man, I don't even hardly know them motherfuckers." The man released Faith, calmly stepped over Jerry, and walked through the door.

"You okay?" the teenager asked Faith breathlessly. She nodded, too shook up to even speak.

"Man, let's get out of here. Someone probably called the pigs with all the yelling this girl did," Shafik said as he slipped the knife into his jacket pocket.

"What you going to do?" the boy asked Faith.

"I'm going home," Faith said weakly.

"Good, I'll walk you." He grabbed Faith's arm and pulled her toward the roof door before she could say anything else. No one spoke as the three of them ran down the five flights of stairs and out onto the street. They quickly walked to the corner and then leaned against a car to catch their breath.

"All right, God. That's it for me for tonight. You okay?" Shafik asked after a few minutes.

"Yeah, thanks for getting my back up there, God."

"You know it's like that, little bro. You heading back downtown?"

"Naw, man. I'm going to walk on home," the teenager answered, and then looked at Faith. "Wait a minute, where do you live anyway?"

Faith blinked wildly as she tried to come up with an answer. Despite all that had happened, she still didn't want to go back and live in a house where she faced the same fate that she had on the roof. She couldn't go to Aunt Gloria's house, because she would call her mother.

"Where do you live?" he asked again.

"In Harlem," Faith answered, trying to buy more time to think.

"Where in Harlem, girl?" Shafik asked impatiently.

"Um, 409 Edgecomb Avenue," Faith answered.

"You want me to take her home on the subway, God? I have to go to Harlem anyway." Shafik asked. The teenager was looking at Faith as though he knew she was lying. Faith looked down at the ground to avoid his eyes and suddenly remembered her open blouse. She put her hand in front of herself and wished she had taken the young man's sweater.

"Naw, God, I'll take her home in a cab. You can catch a ride with us," the teenager finally answered. "What's your name, anyway?"

"Faith." She continued to look down at the sidewalk.

"Peace, Faith. I'm Henry, and this here's Shafik." He smiled at her confusion. "Shafik calls me Raheem. Everyone else calls me Henry."

"I wish you'd hurry up and get it together and stop introducing yourself by your slave name. Haven't we taught you anything yet?" Shafik grunted at his young protégé.

"Hi. I mean, peace." Faith reached out her arm to Shafik to shake hands, but the man just shook his head in disbelief.

"Girl, this young god just risked his life for you and all you can say is 'Hi. I mean, peace'? You'd better come better than that," he snapped at her.

"Thank you," Faith mumbled, her eyes returning to the sidewalk.

"Leave her alone, Shafik. It's all good," Henry said. "Hey, Shafik, let her wear your jacket, God. She's shivering."

Faith silently stared out the window during the fifteen-minute ride to Harlem, barely listening to Shafik and Henry's discussion of the fight with Jerry and his crew. She considered jumping out of the cab when it stopped at a light, but she figured the men would run after her since they were so bent on making sure she got home okay. But she didn't think the men would hurt her; heck, they had fought for her after all, and neither one acted like they were going to get fresh. They seemed pretty cool, especially Henry. She stole a glance at him. He was really cute, too. His complexion was dark coffee, with thick eyebrows and only the hint of a mustache. Real cute, she decided. He looked about her age, maybe a year or two older. Definitely still in high school. She quickly turned back to the window when she realized he noticed her staring. No use in giving him any ideas. She wasn't interested in boys. Not even cute boys like him.

When the cab stopped in front of the huge six-story building on

Edgecomb Avenue, Faith quickly opened the cab door and jumped out, yelling a brief "Thanks" behind her.

"Keep the meter running," she heard Henry yell. Damn, she thought, so much for a clean getaway.

"Wait, I'll walk you." Henry gently took hold of her arm as she trotted toward the massive building.

"That's okay. I'll be fine." She turned to him with a smile.

"I just want to make sure." Henry smiled back.

"Well, um, my mother would be upset if she saw a boy walking me home this time of night. You know how mothers are." Faith fumbled for an excuse. As soon as Henry got into the cab, she planned to make a beeline out of the building and back onto the street to find another place, a safe place, to sleep.

"Yeah, I know how mothers are," Henry chuckled. He let go of Faith's arm, but didn't move back toward the waiting taxi.

"Well, good night. And thanks for everything," Faith said hopefully.

"Good night, and you're welcome." Henry still stood there.

"Aren't you going to get back in your cab?" Faith finally asked.

"Yep, as soon you use your key to get in the building." Henry continued to smile at her. "Then I'll know you'll be safe."

Key? Faith swung to face the front door of the lobby. She didn't realize the building was locked.

"Oh, shoot. I must have lost my key," she said hurriedly.

"Well, I'm sure the doorman will let you in." Henry waved toward an old man sitting at a small desk in the lobby, motioning for him to come to the door.

"No, that's okay . . . I don't think I'm going in after all. I think I'm going to . . ." Faith's shoulders suddenly sagged. She was too tired to even think of another lie. Tears welled up in her eyes, and she quickly looked down so Henry wouldn't see.

"Listen, Faith," Henry lifted Faith's chin up and forced her to look at him as he smiled reassuringly, "how about we let Shafik take the cab, and we walk over to Amsterdam Avenue to get something to eat. I'm starved, and I could use the company since you don't seem ready to call it a night, anyway."

Food! Faith hadn't eaten anything that day, and just half a sandwich the day before.

"Well, if you want to," she said, trying not to sound eager, although her stomach grumbled furiously at the thought of eating.

"I want to." He grabbed her by the hand and they walked back to the cab.

"Yo, man, I'm going to take this queen to get something to eat," he said through the open door. "I'ma catch you later, okay?"

"Yeah, okay, but . . ." Shafik started.

"And don't worry, I got this." Henry pulled a ten-dollar bill from his pocket and handed it to the cab driver.

"Yo, God, you know you don't have to do that," Shafik said, though gratitude was written all over his face.

"Don't sweat it, God. I'll talk to you at the meeting. Peace." Henry started to shut the cab door, but changed his mind and poked his head back inside.

"Yo, God. I need a big favor."

"What's that, God?"

"Let me hold your shirt until tomorrow. It's chilly out here."

Shafik laughed and obligingly took off his shirt and handed it to Henry, then the cab pulled off.

"Shall we go?" Henry turned to Faith, giving a slight bow.

"We shall." Faith giggled.

"Then let's kick it!"

It was 4:00 A.M., so most of the restaurants were closed, and

Henry said he didn't like fast food joints, so the two of them walked to 145th Street and Adam Clayton Powell Jr. Boulevard to Sherman's Barbecue Restaurant. She wanted spareribs and spaghetti, but Henry said black folks shouldn't eat swine, so she settled on barbeque chicken and potato salad instead, and Henry ordered the same.

"Where are we going to eat?" she asked as they waited for the food. Sherman's was a take-out restaurant and didn't have tables or chairs.

"Well, how about we eat in the park? We'll make it a midnight picnic. Well, a 4:00 A.M. picnic." Henry grinned.

Henry lived in the Bronx with his mother and an older sister, who was attending Norfolk State University in Virginia, Faith learned over dinner on the wet grass. He was seventeen, and had been the man of the house since his father had died three years earlier from kidney failure. Henry had worshiped his father, an independent construction worker who used to take his son out to job sites, teaching him the trade. ("Mostly I hauled plaster and cement, but he finally taught me some skills," Henry said, laughing.) His favorite rap groups were KRS-1 and Public Enemy. ("I like music with a message.")

He started hanging out with Five Percenters a year after his father died because he liked the message that they were trying to teach. Every black man was God in his own right, and every black woman was a queen who should be treated as such. A black man had to determine his own fate. Since no one was going to help him, people should get the hell out of the way while he helped himself.

Faith was too busy eating to speak much, but she enjoyed listening to Henry. He was one of those people who smiled when he talked, with a huge grin never far behind. And he was polite, too. He didn't tease her about the way she wolfed down her food, and even offered her some of his when she was finished. She declined, although she could have easily eaten three more dinners.

"I bet you have to go to the bathroom," he said when he noticed her fidgeting.

"Yeah, I do." Faith laughed. "But I can hold it for a little while."

"Are you ready to go home yet?"

"No, not really." Faith looked at him to gauge his reaction.

"Okay, come on. I'm taking you home with me." He got up and dusted off his pants, then reached out to help her to her feet.

Faith didn't hesitate. It seemed simple enough. He was now her boyfriend. And, she thought, it's kind of nice having a boyfriend. Especially one who as sweet as Henry—and as cute.

It was surprisingly easy to catch a taxi on Adam Clayton Powell Jr. Boulevard, even at 5:30 in the morning. Dawn was breaking and people were on their way to work. Twenty minutes later, they were back in the Bronx and Henry was ushering her into a neatly furnished, very clean apartment.

"Where's your mother?" she asked after she had used the bathroom. Henry was playing Nintendo on the large television set in the living room.

"Gone. She leaves for work at six." Henry put down the joystick and stood up. "You want to take a shower?"

"Umm . . ." Faith stuttered. Oh wow, she couldn't take a shower with him. He had been her boyfriend for like only an hour. And she had never seen a boy naked, except her little brother when she used to give him baths—and that certainly didn't count.

He headed into the bathroom, then came back out and threw her a fluffy yellow towel and matching washcloth.

"You may as well go first. I'll look in my sister's room for some clothes you can wear."

"Where are we going?" she yelled as he disappeared into a bedroom.

"To school." He reappeared and handed her a large burgundy robe.

"I can't go to my school!" She knew that by now her mother had surely notified the school officials that Faith had run away. If she showed up on school grounds, they'd call her mother—or the police.

"Why not?" Henry looked at her, his brow furrowed in puzzlement.

"Because I just can't! Don't you understand anything?" Faith threw the towel onto the couch and then plopped down beside it, burying her face in her hands as she tried not to cry.

"Well, one thing I do understand is that I've been up all night and I have a geometry test in about an hour. So, if you're not going to go to your school, you're going to have to come with me to mine." Henry shook her gently on the shoulder. "Now hurry up and take your shower so I'm not late."

Faith looked up. "Oh yeah? They're going to just let me walk into your class while you take your test?"

"Girl, this is DeWitt Clinton we're talking about. You think the teachers even know the names of the students in their class?" Henry chuckled. "Now hurry up."

"Okay, but can I ask you one real quick question?"

"Make it quick."

"Am I your girlfriend?" Faith gathered up the towel and the robe as she asked the question, so she didn't have to look at Henry as he answered.

She finally looked up when he didn't respond, and found him staring at her, his head cocked to one side.

"Well?" she asked almost defiantly.

"Do you want to be my girlfriend?" he finally asked.

She looked back down at her hands. "Yeah," she mumbled.

"How old are you, Faith?" he asked quietly.

"Fifteen."

He stared at her for a few more seconds, and then broke out in a grin. "You can be my girlfriend when you're sixteen. Now hurry up so I'm not late for my test."

She stared at him as he disappeared back into the bedroom. This, she thought, has got to be the weirdest day of my life.

"I think I aced it. See, Queen, you're my good-luck charm. Boy, I know I'm going to get an A in that class. I need it, too. I think I'm only averaging a B in Spanish. Maybe a B-plus. I need to bring you with me next week for my Spanish exam." Henry was darn near strutting with pride as he walked back from school to the apartment. He slowed down when he noticed Faith struggling to keep up with him.

"I'm sorry. I walk fast when I'm excited," he said. "You okay?"

"Fine. I'm just tired, I guess," Faith said apologetically. She was as excited for him as he was for himself. Not only a cute boyfriend, but a smart one, too. And it didn't matter if he thought she was too young; she'd change his mind.

"So, girl, I've been doing all the talking. What about you?" he asked.

"What about me?" she asked suspiciously.

"Well, where do you go to school, for starters? When you do go, that is." He chuckled.

"Hunter High," she said simply.

"Hunter? Really? You have to test to get into there. That's a really good school." He whistled his appreciation.

"Yeah, it's okay." She fell silent.

"Well . . ." he said after a few moments, "what's your favorite subject?"

"Literature," she answered quickly and truthfully. Faith had turned to books to escape the nightmare of living with Papa. She would bring the family shopping cart with her to the library to haul all of her books home. There was supposed to be a limit of six books per person, but the librarians let her slide. She seldom watched television or went to the movies—reading was her escape. She used to love the Black Stallion books by Walter Farley, and the *Lad: A Dog* series by Albert Payson Terhune, and everything ever written by Charles Dickens and Mark Twain. Then a librarian recommended a collection of short stories by Langston Hughes called *Simply Heaven*, and Faith was hooked. She read all of Hughes's stories, plays, poems, and essays, then every biography she could find on the man. Then she moved on to the other Harlem Renaissance writers like Jean Toomer, Dorothy West, Walter Thurman, and Nella Larsen.

"Yeah, I like literature, too. African-American literature especially," he said as he unlocked the door to his apartment. "My favorite poet is Claude McKay."

Faith tapped him on the shoulder, and when he turned to face her, she stepped back and began to recite.

> *If we must die, let it not be like hogs,*
> *Hunted and penned in an inglorious spot,*
> *While round us bark the mad and hungry dogs,*
> *Making their mock at our accursed lot.*

He looked at her in astonishment. "You know Claude McKay?"

She nodded with a smile, proud to have pleased him. "He's one of my favorite writers, too."

"Really? Who else do you like?" he asked with genuine interest.

"I'm not going to tell you. You have to guess." Faith grinned. "But here's a hint."

> My old man's a white old man,
> My old mother's black,
> If I ever cursed my white old man
> I'd take my curses back
> If I every cursed my black old mother
> And wished she were in Hell
> I'm sorry for that evil wish
> And now I wish her well

Henry reached over and covered Faith's mouth, continuing the poem for her.

> My old man died in a big fine house
> My ma died in a shack
> I wonder where I'm going to die
> Being neither white nor black

"Langston Hughes!" Henry beamed. "That's 'The Cross,' right?"

"I can't believe you knew that one. I always stump people with that!" Faith said excitedly.

"And I can't believe you know Harlem Renaissance writers." Henry grinned back as they walked inside the apartment. You're a little braniac, huh?"

"No, I'm just a Harlem Renaissance fiend. I like Richard Wright and Ralph Ellison, too. And guess what," she said, almost hopping up and down with excitement.

"What?" he asked with a small laugh.

"I'm born on James Weldon Johnson's birthday!" She beamed with pride.

"Well, now you guess what." He grinned.

"What?"

"I'm born on February first."

Faith's hands flew to her mouth. "You're born on Langston Hughes's birthday? Oh my God, that's so awesome."

"Nah, I lied to see your reaction." Henry grinned, and the two of them doubled over with laughter.

"Okay, you haven't gotten any sleep," he said after they calmed down. He glanced at his watch. "Ma'am won't be home until five, and it's only one-thirty now. You can take a nap while I get some studying done."

"Who's Ma'am?" Faith asked. Just the mention of sleep made her eyes heavy.

"We call our mother 'Ma'am.' You know, like 'Yes, ma'am' or 'Yes, sir.' You want something to eat before you crash?" He led her to a small bedroom with pastel walls and pink, ruffled curtains that matched the sheets on the two twin-size beds. "I can make you a sandwich, if you'd like."

"No, that's okay." Faith eyed the bed. "Is it okay if I lay down in these clothes?"

"Yeah, no problem." He leaned against the doorjamb and looked at her thoughtfully. "But what is going to be a problem is what we're going to do with you when Ma'am comes home. You're still not ready to go home, I guess?"

Faith sat down on one of the beds and shook her head.

"And I guess you're not ready to tell me why?"

She shook her head again.

"And you don't really live at 409 Edgecomb Avenue, do you?"

Faith shook her head again.

"I didn't think so. You picked that building because it was a Harlem Renaissance writer hangout, and like you said, you're a Harlem Renaissance fiend." He grinned at his cleverness.

"Well, I am going to live there one day." Faith pouted. "James Weldon Johnson lived there, you know. And so did Duke Ellington."

"And so did Bill 'Bojangles' Robinson. But you don't live there now, and you won't say where you live, and that's what matters right now." Henry sighed. "Okay, you go ahead and lay down, and I'll wake you up in a couple of hours. We'll figure something out then."

"You're not going to stay here with me?" Faith asked anxiously.

"I'm just going to be down the hall in the living room, studying. Just come on out if you need something."

"But we aren't finished talking yet." Faith tried, unsuccessfully, to stifle a yawn.

"A couple of hours ago I could barely get you to say your name, and now you don't want to shut up." He laughed. "Get some sleep. We'll talk when you wake up."

"Um, okay. Is this your sister's room?" Faith asked, looking around.

"Yep."

"Why are there two beds?" She really didn't care, but she wanted to keep him talking so he wouldn't leave.

"I used to have two sisters." He shrugged, trying to act nonchalant, but Faith noticed a cloud pass across his face.

"*Used* to have two sisters? What happened to the other one?" she asked carefully.

He paused, and his face grew dark. "She died last year. Some guy threw her off a roof." He walked over and ruffled her hair. "Get some sleep now, okay? We'll talk more later. I promise."

. . .

Bleeeeep!

Faith didn't bother responding to the blaring car horn, which couldn't be directed at her this time since she was safely on the sidewalk in front of her apartment building. She smiled through the glass-paneled front door as the security guard slowly got up from his desk in the lobby to let her in, as he had every day since she and Henry moved in. This was the same apartment building that James Weldon Johnson, Duke Ellington, and Bill "Bojangles" Robinson had lived in decades before.

Henry was eighteen and Faith was only sixteen at the time they moved into the spacious two-bedroom apartment. Henry's mother had died of a heart attack the year before, and his sister didn't seem to care one way or the other what Henry did, but Miss Irene had been scandalized. Especially since Faith had reluctantly admitted that Henry's main source of income was selling cocaine.

"Mom, he's only doing it to support his family. His mother couldn't make ends meet on her salary, and he didn't want his sister to have to drop out of college," Faith pleaded. "And it's not like he's going to do it forever. He's got goals. He's going to become an accountant. You know he's real good at math."

"I'm not having it," Miss Irene huffed. "I don't want you around anyone selling drugs. I've raised you better than that."

"You didn't say anything when Allen was selling drugs," Faith snapped. She was seldom outright rude to her mother, but this was important, in her mind.

"That's different. It wasn't like he was making anywhere near the money Henry must be making to put a sister through college," Miss Irene snapped back.

"Oh, Henry is more successful than Allen, so that makes him a worse guy?" Faith griped. "That's a double standard. You didn't say anything when Allen was doing it because he was buying you stuff."

Miss Irene finally calmed down when Henry invited her to dinner and told her that he intended to send Faith to college, as well as marry her as soon as she turned eighteen or, if Miss Irene preferred, as soon as Faith got her bachelor's degree. He would be well into his own career, he assured Miss Irene, and would be able to support them.

He also pointed out that Faith had run away three times in the two years he'd known her. "She never told me why she's so unhappy at home, but if you insist that she stay there, I understand," he lied. "But of course, I'll do my best to find out what's troubling her and do what I can to rectify it, so we both know she's safe."

Miss Irene said she'd think about it. The next day Papa came home with a bloodied lip and a broken arm and no explanation for either. Miss Irene had a sudden change of heart and allowed Faith to move in the following week.

"Afternoon, Miss Freeman. Kinda chilly out dere, ain't it?"

"Hey Mr. Carpenter." Faith flashed a broad smile at the man who looked to be in his sixties. He was still fresh with the young ladies, though. He had even tried to hit on Faith when she and Henry first moved into the building, but Henry sat him down for a "man-to-man talk," and the security guard had been nothing but respectful since. "I hope your son's going to pick you up today. It's not walking weather."

"Yeah, he said he'd be around here. Should be any minute now," Mr. Carpenter answered as Faith took out her keys to check the mailbox.

"Mr. Prince done picked up the mail."

"Dang, I was hoping to make it in before him." Faith bit her lip.

"Well, you did and you didn't." Mr. Carpenter chuckled as he shuffled back to the lobby desk. "He done went out agin 'bout twenty minutes ago."

Faith looked at her watch—4:00 P.M. The walk from her mother's house had taken longer than she thought. She could forget about taking a nap. She wanted to cook a special dinner for Henry. One, because he was leaving for Chicago in the morning, and two, because she wanted him to be in a good mood when she told him that Hope was going to be staying with them for a while. Hopefully, her twin would get in later than her boyfriend.

7

What about Wesley Snipes?"

"Nope. He's ruggedly handsome, but not cute like you."

"You trying to say I'm not ruggedly handsome?" Henry pursed his lips, trying to make believe he was hurt, but Faith knew he was joking. He was frowning, but the twinkle never left his eye.

"I didn't say that, baby. You're ruggedly handsome and cute. He's just ruggedly handsome," she said soothingly as she rubbed her hand over his bare chest and lightly flicked her tongue below his ear. They had just finished making love, but it was so good that now that Faith was rested up, she wanted more.

Henry, being Henry, playfully pushed her away. He wanted to finish playing the "Would You Dump Me For . . ." game. It was her fault, in a way. She's the one who started it when they first began going together.

"What about Denzel?"

"He's married."

"But what if he weren't?"

"Nope, he's too bland. He's handsome and cute, but he's not sexy enough for me."

The scent of jasmine hung heavily in the room, which was dark except for the ivory lamp on Faith's night table. The night was quiet, or as quiet as you could expect for an apartment in a city as noisy as New York. It was cold outside, so many of the night dwellers who would normally still be out and making noise at 1:30 A.M. were at home, theirs or someone else's, trying to stay warm. The superintendent, old Mr. Johnson, had turned down the heat in the building just an hour before, so the old-fashioned steam radiator in Henry and Faith's huge bedroom was still warm and would be for a few hours, thanks in part to the heavily embroidered floor-length drapes that insulated the windows against noise as well as weather. At the foot of the bed rested a neatly folded champagne-colored satin bed comforter, in case it got chilly during the night. But at the moment, the champagne satin sheets were more than enough to keep the couple warm.

"Michael Jackson?"

"Very funny." Faith tried to swat him with a pillow, but he grabbed it from her hand and swatted her instead.

"Lay down and answer my questions, woman!" he growled. Faith took the other pillow and tried to smother him, but he managed to grab it. Laughing, she tugged back with all her strength, even bracing her legs against his chest for more power. He grinned broadly, which should have given her fair warning that he was up to something, then suddenly let go of the pillow, and she rocketed to the floor. He scooted over to the edge of the bed and laughed.

"Serves you right!" he said.

"You make me sick." Faith got up slowly, feigning an injury to her lower back. When his laughter turned into a look of concern, she pounced on him and managed to get the pillow over his face for a whole tenth of a second before he flipped her. Suddenly she was on her back in the bed and he was straddling her.

"Hmm," she said as she licked her lips while thrusting her nude hips up against his naked flesh, "this is more like it."

"Still trying to change the subject, huh?" He leaned down and kissed her on the forehead, then lay back down beside her, propped on an elbow—ready to restart his interrogation. All she could do was sigh.

"I know who you'd dump me for in a hot minute!" he finally said triumphantly.

"And who's that?" Faith let out another sigh.

"L.L. Cool J!"

Faith propped herself up on an elbow like Henry. Hmm . . . L.L. Cool J . . . that's a hard one. After all, he's a really good-looking brother and he . . . A vengeful pillow interrupted her thoughts.

"You would really leave me for L.L. Cool J!" Henry tried to roll Faith out of the bed, and Faith clung to the headboard to prevent another fall, but they were both enveloped with laughter.

"I didn't say I would!" Faith hollered.

"You took too long to think about it!" He was trying to unclench her hands from the headboard while continuing to shove her with his feet.

"No, no, I would never leave you for L.L. Cool J!" Faith hollered again. "Really!"

Henry stopped and looked at Faith, his feet, though, were still poised against her body for a quick shove. "You swear?"

"I swear."

"Promise?"

"I promise."

Henry relaxed his body and moved closer to her, giving her a small kiss on the lips as he caressed the back of her neck.

"Even if he walked through the door with a five-carat diamond ring set in platinum?"

"Even then." Faith lightly kissed him on the chin as his breaths started getting deeper, signaling his arousal. Faith reached down between his legs to be sure. Yep, he was getting aroused.

"You wouldn't leave me for anybody? Ever?" he asked as he started playing with her nipples.

"Nobody, baby," Faith answered in a husky voice. She waited for two beats, before she pulled his head to hers and then whispered in his ear, "Except Robert De Niro."

"Robert De Niro!" He pulled away with an incredulous look on his face. "You have the hots for The Godfather?" He started laughing hysterically. Not that she could explain why, but Faith found it rather insulting. Faith punched him in the chest to make him stop.

"He's old as all hell," he managed to get out.

"He's sexy as all hell." Faith leaned back on the bed and licked her lips, looking out of the corner of her eye to make sure Henry noticed. She was hoping to get him back in the pseudojealousy mode. Even that was better than him laughing at her possible pick for his replacement.

"Please," Henry snorted. "He's old enough to be your father. And he's white to boot."

"He's not white."

"Pardon me?"

"Well, okay, technically he is white, but he's also an honorary black man," Faith said with a patronizing shrug at Henry's ignorance of this common knowledge.

"I see, and when was he given this honor? And by whom? The NAACP? The Rainbow Coalition? The Congressional Black Caucus?" The expression on Henry's face indicated that he thought the whole thing was hilarious, but his interest seemed piqued. Faith definitely had him going. She managed to stifle a giggle before answering.

"Me, Mommy, and Hope."

"Oh really!" Henry hooted. "Oh well, that certainly makes it official."

"It most certainly does," Faith said with a solemn nod of her head.

"And what, may I ask, makes Mr. Robert De Niro eligible for the distinguished title of Honorary Black Man?" Henry grinned. "Because he cohabitates with black women?"

"No, not just that. A lot of white men go for black women, but it does help that he's just so nonchalant about it," Faith said slowly. "I mean, he's not one of those white guys who only go after black women who are big stars. Or worse, one that goes with a black woman and starts hanging out exclusively with blacks and trying to speak ebonics and crap."

"So it doesn't have anything to do with his choice of women? Okay, then why?"

"I don't know." She giggled. "We couldn't figure out why either. I guess we all thought he was too damn sexy not to be black."

"Oh? So if a white man is sexy then you guys consider him an honorary black?"

"Oh no!" Faith said in mock astonishment. "There are plenty of sexy white men who aren't black. Alec Baldwin is sexy as all hell. So is Sean Connery and Pierce Brosnan. But they're still white."

"They're sexy, but not black, huh?"

"Nope."

"But Robert De Niro is sexy and black?"

"Yep."

"Give me a break," Henry laughed. "You and your mom and your sister are the craziest women I've ever met."

"But you love us anyway." Faith snuggled up close to him.

"Well, I love you. And I guess you could say I love your mom." Henry lightly stroked her shoulders, but a sudden change in his mood was evident.

"And Hope?" Faith asked almost coyly.

"I like her a helluva lot, but you've got to admit she's a pain in the ass," Henry snorted.

"Yeah, I know she is. But she's still my sister," Faith said soothingly.

"She's a user, is what she is." Henry moved Faith's arm away, leaned back on the bed, and stared at the ceiling. "I don't understand why she has to stay with us every time your mother puts her out. Why can't your brother Allen take her in for a change?"

"Because he lives with his girlfriend and she doesn't want anything to do with Hope."

Henry grunted. "And I do?"

"Yeah, you do, Henry, you just don't like some of the things she does—neither do I—but you know she's really a nice person. She's just got to get herself together and . . ."

"You know, Faith . . . you need to just stop it." Henry suddenly got up and pulled on the pajama pants that had been tossed on a nearby brass chair, then plopped back in the bed, pulling the sheet over him. Even as Faith concentrated on his anger about Hope staying with them, she felt a fleeting pang of disappointment knowing she wasn't going to be getting any more loving that night.

"Listen, I don't know that Hope is a nice person. I like her, she's funny as hell, but I'm not all that sure she's a nice person. So don't put words in my mouth, okay?" he said gruffly. "Got that?"

"Got it." Dang, he didn't have to act so mean about it, she thought. Faith grabbed part of the sheet and pulled it over her as she turned her back to him. He immediately tapped her on the shoulder.

"Turn around," he demanded.

"Go to hell." He just dissed my sister, denied me sex, and now he's going to order me around, too? I don't think so.

"Fine, I'll talk to your back." He didn't even seem fazed, which pissed Faith off even more.

"Hope's a crack addict. She lies, she steals, and she sleeps with guys for money, and I haven't even got to the worst stuff," Henry continued. "She also . . ."

"She doesn't steal!" Faith whirled around to confront him.

"Hey! Stop yelling. Your family is the most hollering folks I know." Henry's voice softened as if to change the tone of their conversation. "But, baby, shoplifting is stealing, and how many times have we had to go down and bail her out of jail for boosting?"

"Well, at least she doesn't steal from people." Faith grumbled.

"Granted. At least not that we know of."

Faith shot him a dirty look, then once more showed him the back of her head, hoping he'd get the message and leave her alone. No such luck.

"And she sleeps with every man your mother brings home," he continued. "Now, in my book, that's not a very nice person."

"You know she's only doing that because of what happened to her as a kid," Faith snapped.

"Well, she's a grown-ass adult now!"

"Okay, you've made your point." Faith turned around to face him. "But none of that has anything to do with the fact that she's my sister, she doesn't have anywhere to stay, and I'm not going to let her sleep in the street!" she shouted in his face.

"Faith, I'm right here. Stop yelling," Henry said in an irritated voice.

"Then stop talking about my sister!"

"Then stop letting her shack up here," Henry said.

"She's got no money. She's got no job. She's got nowhere to go!" Faith jumped out of bed and stomped over to Henry's side of the mattress and yanked the pillow from beneath his head. *"What the fuck do you suggest she do?"*

Henry jumped up out of the bed so fast Faith had to stumble backward to get out of his way. His nostrils were flared and he was breathing hard, as if he were in the middle of a fistfight.

"You know what, Faith? I really don't have any fucking suggestions, okay?" he said slowly through clenched teeth. He stood there for a moment staring at her before reaching for the comforter and heading toward the bedroom door. He opened the door to leave, then suddenly swung back around to face her.

"Scratch that . . . I do have one suggestion," he said with a sneer. "If that bitch can sell pussy to buy crack, I suggest she sell pussy to pay rent on her own apartment. Then she can stay the hell out of ours."

"Fuck you, Henry!" Faith threw the pillow at him and looked around to see what else she could grab. She reached for the alarm clock, but the bedroom door slammed shut, and Henry was gone. She stalked over to the door and flung it open. "And you know what else? I *would* dump you for L.L. Cool J! And for Al Pacino, too!"

"Wake up, it's your turn to apologize!"

Faith reluctantly pulled the comforter from over her head and peered sleepily at Henry, who was standing over her, already showered, shaven, and half-dressed. She leaned up on her elbows and peered at the alarm clock, lying face-up on the nightstand where she left it the night before, and groaned—5:15 A.M.

"Why are you up so early? And why are you getting me up so early?" Faith grumbled as she got out of bed.

"My plane leaves at nine, and I wanted to have some breakfast and pick up some files from the office for my meeting in Chicago." Henry was standing in front of the mirror, tying his tie in a Windsor knot as he talked. "And I want my apology before I leave. My cab's going to be here soon, so you'd better hurry up."

"I thought your plane left at ten." Faith was stalling for time. She and Henry had made a pact shortly after moving in together that they would take turns apologizing after a fight, no matter who had started the altercation. They didn't have to say they were wrong about the issue, just that they were sorry it had escalated to a fight. But she was sure she had apologized last. Hadn't she? She sure didn't want to be apologizing this time. She tried to remember the last fight they had. Oh yeah, last month, when her mother had asked for seven hundred dollars for a hot water heater that shouldn't have cost more than three hundred. Henry was right. Damn it, it was her turn to apologize.

"I told you last night that my flight was changed, Faith."

"Oh, yeah."

"Umm, and my apology?" Henry was slipping into his dark blue suit pants while he looked at her expectantly. She sighed, then walked over and stood in front of him.

"Henry, I love you very much . . ." she said with lowered eyes.

"I love you, too, baby."

"And I'm really very sorry about our fight last night," she continued. "I hope you'll forgive me for allowing things to get out of hand like that." There, she had made the required speech. She looked up at him, expecting to see the gloating look he usually wore in these circumstances. Instead, he pulled her close to him and kissed her. Hard. And long.

"What was that all about?" she asked when he finally released her.

"That was because I didn't think you were going to apologize," he grinned.

"What do you mean? It was my turn, wasn't it?" she asked suddenly suspicious.

"Oh, no, it was your turn. Don't get me wrong. But I know how you are about your sister," he said as he pulled his suspenders over his shoulders. "In all these years, if you think about it, we've never had an argument about her. I know she's probably the only person in this world you love more than me."

"So you think I'd dump you for my sister?" Faith grinned.

"In a Harlem second." Henry playfully poked her on the forehead. "But it's never going to come to that because I'm not stupid enough to make you choose." He took her by the hand, walked over to the bed, and sat down. She sat down next to him.

"Baby, let me tell you something. Hope has some issues, and I know they stem from some real problems she had growing up—"

"That's so true! And that's why I've been trying—"

Henry ignored the interruption and continued. "It's obvious the reason she jumps in bed with all of your mother's boyfriends is because she really resents your mother for not throwing your stepfather out after she found out what was going on. Hell, I resent your mother for it, and I wasn't the one molested. But she's got to deal with those issues. And while I understand that you feel sorry for her and want to help her, you have to understand that you've become an enabler, babe."

"What do you mean? I've never given her money for drugs," Faith said as her hands flew to her hips.

"Calm down, we're not going to fight again, okay? But I really think we should talk about this," Henry said soothingly. "I'm not talking about the drugs right now. I'm talking about Hope never having to take any kind of responsibility for her life because she knows that whatever happens, you'll help her out. You'll pay her bail when she gets busted for shoplifting. You'll jump up and hit anyone who threatens her. You'll take her in when she has nowhere to go—"

"But that's what I'm supposed to do," Faith interrupted. "That's what sisters are supposed to do for each other."

"If Hope were mentally healthy, I'd agree. But, baby, as long as you're bailing her out of the jams she puts herself in, she's going to keep getting into them. Don't you see that? She knows you're going to bail her out of jail, so she's going to keep shoplifting. She knows that you're not going to let her become homeless, so she doesn't have to get a job and pay rent. You're allowing her—enabling her—to continue living a reckless and unhealthy lifestyle. You don't realize it, but you're doing more harm than good."

Faith closed her eyes and sighed, knowing that Henry was right. "So what do you suggest I do?" she finally asked, dismally. "Tell her I changed my mind and she can't stay here?"

"No, not at all." Henry folded his hands over Faith's. "I'm suggesting that you let her stay here, but set some ground rules."

"Such as?"

"One, that she look for a job. And two, once she gets that job, she has to start looking around for her own place. And I don't mean moving back in with your mother, either. You've got to make her understand that she has to learn to stand on her own two feet."

"You think it's okay for her to stay here until she gets a job and saves enough money to pay for security and rent on an apartment," Faith asked in an incredulous tone.

"Aw, naw . . . I certainly don't think that. But . . . if she gets a job, we can help her look for an apartment within her salary range, and we can loan her the money for the security and first month's rent," Henry said patiently. "It can be a long-term loan. Maybe we'd have her pay back only fifty dollars a month or something. But the thing is, we'd be helping her move toward independence. That's all I'm asking, baby."

"Henry?"

"Yes, baby?"

"You do like Hope, don't you?"

Henry sighed. "Of course I do, that's part of the problem. Everyone likes Hope because she's so damn lovable. But she needs help, and you're the only person who really has a chance to get through to her. So, it may seem like I'm being mean, but I'm just trying to help you see what you've got to do to help your sister."

Faith closed her eyes again and shook her head. When she opened them her tears were evident. "Dang, Henry, what did I ever do to deserve a man like you? I love you so much."

8

Henry kissed Faith on the forehead, looked into her eyes, then gave her a quick peck on the cheek. "You think we have time for breakfast before I get out of here? Maybe just some toast and coffee?"

"Maybe." Faith stood on her tiptoes and nibbled his ear. "And maybe we have time for a quick something else. Hmm?"

"Shit!" a woman's voice cried out from the foyer, just as they heard a vase crash onto the hardwood floor.

"Maybe not." Henry sighed, then shrugged his shoulders and gave a slight chuckle.

"Hope, is that you?" It was a stupid question since Faith had recognized her sister's voice, but an automatic one. She also wanted to ask if it was the $650 white porcelain vase that stood on the end table by the door that had just shattered, or the simple vase holding the flowers that Henry had brought home the night before, but decided against it. She'd find out as soon as she walked out of the bedroom anyway.

"Yeah, it's me!" Hope appeared in the bedroom doorway, her eyes were glazed and stance unsteady—sure signs she was high on something. There was no trace of alcohol on her breath. Had to be crack, then. "I'm sorry but I knocked over that white vase when I walked in. But don't worry, I'll pay for it. I know it musta been cheap as easy as it shattered and stuff."

"Don't even worry about it." Henry tried to keep his voice light, but Faith knew he was irritated. The vase had been their first purchase for their new apartment when the two of them were just teenagers.

"I'm sorry about that," Faith whispered in his ear.

"Hey, Hope, why don't you go grab some sleep in the guest room and I'll wake you up later so we can talk," she said, turning to her sister, who was bobbing her head up and down to music only she could hear.

"Yeah, okay." Hope started shuffling off, but then slowly turned around. "Hey, is there anything to eat? I'm starved."

Henry grinned. "Your sister was just getting ready to fix us some breakfast, weren't you baby?"

"Yeah, just toast and coffee, though," Faith grumbled as she grabbed her brown terry cloth robe from a hook on the bedroom door.

"Yeah, I could use some toast and coffee," Hope said as she trailed behind Faith into the kitchen. "More toast than coffee, though."

"Henry's being a sweetheart, but I know he's pissed," Faith said when they were out of earshot. "Why didn't you ring the doorbell instead of just walking in like that? We could have been in the middle of doing it on the living room couch or something. Or Henry could have been walking around in his drawers."

Hope shrugged. "I seen men in their drawers before, you know."

"Well, I ain't planning on you seeing my man in his drawers,"

Faith snapped as she bustled around the kitchen, opening and shutting cabinet doors for no reason, trying to calm herself down. She had been so sure she was going to be the recipient of some make-up loving—well, maybe a make-up quickie—until Hope had come busting through the door.

"And anyway, I was just trying to be considerate," Hope mumbled. "What if you guys were asleep? Most people are this early in the morning. I just ain't wanna wake you up and stuff."

"And man, why do you have to come into this house all high like this? Knocking down the vase and everything."

"I ain't high," Hope said weakly.

"Like hell you aren't."

"Well, I ain't all that high. I'm coming down and stuff." Hope shrugged her shoulders. "I only had a couple of quick hits last night. I ain't know y'all were going to be up and stuff." Hope yawned. "I was just going to come in and go to sleep. I figured by the time I woke up I woulda slept off my high and ya'll wouldn'ta never know and stuff."

Faith started the coffee maker and set the toaster, then looked in the refrigerator for some orange juice. "I guess we have to set some house rules while you're here, Hope. Get in at a decent hour, ring the doorbell when you do, and don't be coming in here high. And"—she slammed the refrigerator for emphasis—"don't even think about getting high up in this apartment. And I mean that." Faith didn't bother to tell Hope not to bring crackheads around. She was terrified when she saw how bad Henry had beat the trick she'd brought over to the apartment a few years before. The look in her eyes said that she thought he was going to beat her, too, but that just wasn't Henry's style. Since then, Hope did have the decency to try to keep her drugs and whoring undercover, which was why she turned tricks in Queens rather than in Harlem.

Hope sat at the kitchen table, her head propped up on her elbow, humming and strumming her fingers on the wood while Faith talked and fixed scrambled eggs.

"And don't think you're going to be coming in here every morning and just going to bed. If Henry and I have to get up and go to work every morning, you're sure as hell getting up and going somewhere," Faith said as she buttered Hope and Henry's toast. "We're not running a hotel here, you know."

"Okay. Whatever."

"In fact, I think it's about high time you started looking for a job," Faith said as she sat down at the table.

"Hey, Baby Girl, why don't you whip up some pancakes or French toast or something," Hope said as she started stuffing the toast in her mouth. "Toast and eggs ain't gonna fill me up."

"Did you hear what I just said, Hope?" Faith demanded.

"Yeah, yeah, yeah, I'm going to look for a job." Hope sighed.

"Did I hear someone say they're looking for a job?" Henry walked into the kitchen and tossed the *New York Times* classifieds on the table before sitting down.

"Oh, you're so helpful." Hope cut her eyes at him.

"I aim to please." Henry winked at Faith, who smiled to see that he was back in his usual jolly mood.

"Anyway, I don't have no clothes to go job hunting," Hope mumbled.

"What's that? I can't hear you." Henry reached over and pinched her shoulder.

"Damn, why you gotta be pinching me?" Hope tried to reach over and slap Henry on the back of the head, but he ducked.

"Just making sure you're awake." Henry grinned. "Hey, Faith, my trip's been canceled." Henry loosened his tie and leaned back in his chair.

"Oh, and why's that?" Faith raised her eyebrows.

"The airports are snowed in." Henry took a sip of his coffee. "Hopefully they'll be open tomorrow, if not the day after. I'm almost finished with this project and I know the publisher wants to get an answer one way or the other before the end of the year so he can make budgeting decisions for the new year."

"So, how does it look? Are you guys going to invest in his company?" Faith asked.

"I'm going to recommend that we do. His business proposal isn't the hottest, but that's only because he got his brother-in-law to put it together for him instead of going to a professional," Henry answered. "The proposal is sound, and the guy is a marketing genius. He can recognize really good first-time authors and he promotes the hell out of their books with the little money he has set aside for promotion. But he's only been able to promote them just enough to catch the eye of the big publishers, who turn around and buy the publishing rights, and then make a mint when they hit big because they now have a major promotional machine behind them."

"They really do come out with some good books," Faith admitted as she took a bite of toast. "I've just never offered them any of my authors because they can't afford to pay advances."

"Well, that may soon change." Henry grinned.

"Hey, hey, stop with all the shop talk at the kitchen table." Hope threw a piece of toast at Henry.

"Don't interrupt when grown folks are talking." Henry swatted her with the newspaper. Hope then flicked a spoonful of scrambled eggs in his direction.

Faith smiled and shook her head as she watched the two people she loved most in the world act like complete idiots at the breakfast table. "I hope you know I'm not cleaning up this mess," she said to neither one of them in particular.

"Hope will clean it up; she doesn't have anything else to do," Henry said.

"Why I gotta clean up? You started it!" Hope replied. "And you just said you ain't gotta go to work today."

"No, I didn't. I said my trip was canceled. I still have to go to the office."

"Liar!"

"Shut up!"

"You shut up!"

Henry reached over to swat Hope on the head again, and when she tried to duck, he swatted her nose instead.

"Achoo!" Hope rubbed her nose and looked at Henry accusingly.

"Gesundheit!" he said.

"Gesundheit, my ass." Hope sucked her teeth. "You probably don't even know what that means."

"It means 'God bless you' in German." Henry smirked.

"No it doesn't, smart-ass."

"Yes, it does, stupid."

"You're the one who's stupid stupid," Hope said triumphantly. "Gesundheit is the name of the German scientist who invented sneezing."

"You're out of your mind." Henry laughed.

"Yes it is! Isn't it, Faith!" Hope looked around at her sister, who was sitting in her chair, silently cracking up.

"Hope, I don't believe you . . . you . . ." Faith was laughing so hard she couldn't speak.

"What? What?" Hope frowned at her sister, then turned back to Henry. "Way back in medieval times, there was a German scientist who was trying to come up with a medicine that would fix all the sicknesses in the world. And everyone in the world knew what he was trying to do, and they were all rooting him on and stuff. So while he was trying to figure out how to make this medicine, he invented this powder—a whole bunch of it—and even though it wasn't the medicine, he figured he could turn it into the medicine. But before he finished, one of helpers dropped the thing the powder was in and it floated out the window and spread all over the world. And people, when they sniffed it, they started sneezing. And they were so mad at him that every time they sneezed they'd say 'Gesundheit' really pissed and shit—because they were blaming him. And the powder stayed in the atmosphere forever, and that's why people still sneeze today, and that's why they say Gesundheit."

Henry looked at Hope and shook his head.

"Where the hell did you come up with that story?" He chuckled.

"Faith told me!" Hope looked at her sister for confirmation. By this time, Faith was laughing so hard she was gasping for air. She was waving her hands, trying to compose herself enough to speak, but couldn't.

"Faith, I know you didn't tell this girl that crock of shit." Henry started hooting in laughter.

Hope looked back and forth at the two of them in bewilderment. "What? What?" she demanded.

"Hope, oh my God," Faith finally managed to get out. "You still believe that after all these years?"

"Why shouldn't I?"

"Henry, when Hope and I were seven years old, she asked me what 'Gesundheit' meant and I didn't know." Faith was still howling with laughter as she spoke. "I didn't want to admit I didn't know, because Hope thought I was the smartest person in the world. So I just made up that story. I didn't remember it until just now." Faith started hooting. "How was I supposed to know she would still believe it at twenty-nine!" Henry and Faith both howled with laughter.

Hope looked at Faith in amazement and shook her head. "Damn.

And all these years, whenever someone said 'Gesundheit' I told them that story. No wonder they looked at me like I was crazy." She started chuckling, then burst into laughter herself. "Faith, you ain't shit!"

"I know!" Faith got up still laughing and hugged her sister, who was laughing so hard they both slid on the floor.

"Mmph," Henry said as he picked up the financial section of *The New York Times*. "Ya'll are the craziest women I've ever met."

9

I told you your brothers weren't coming."

Faith shrugged her shoulders sympathetically as she poured her mother a large glass of Manischewitz Cream White Concord wine. "I never said they were, Mommy."

"You'd think they would want to come over and see me, since they know what I'm going through right now." Miss Irene sat on the side of the bed, wringing her hands. Even through the glasses, Faith could tell that her mother's eyes were red and puffy. Faith involuntarily winced and turned away, pretending to busy herself by wiping a water spot off of the night table.

"I think I intimidated him. Ronald wasn't the brightest person, you know, and I think he was threatened by my intelligence," Miss Irene said dismally as she took a large swallow of the wine. "He was always complaining about my reading all the time and doing crossword puzzles while we were in bed."

"That's probably it, Mommy," Faith said soothingly. "A lot of men are intimidated by smart women."

"Yeah." Miss Irene sighed and took another sip. "And you know he didn't like all the drama that's always going on in the house. The tenants upstairs fighting and carrying on like they don't have good sense. And then they always come to me to straighten things out. It's amazing that Ronald lasted as long as he did." She put her glass down on the night table that Faith had just wiped, then snatched a fresh tissue from the box on the bed next to her and pushed her glasses away from her face so she could dab at her eyes, causing Faith to once again turn away.

"I hate that you have to see me like this, sweetie," Miss Irene said through her sniffles. "I'm really trying to keep it together, baby."

Faith patted her mother on her back. "I know, Mommy. It's okay. I'm here for you. I know how it is."

"No you don't, baby." Miss Irene's back heaved while she tried to keep from bursting into tears as she had so many times that evening. "You have no idea. Henry is the only man you've had and he's never left you, thank God. But you have no idea what I'm going through."

But I've seen you go through it so many times, Faith thought as she continued to rub her mother's shoulders and back. First when Daddy died, then when Papa left, and when . . .

"You know, I was the one doing the leaving before I put on all this weight," Miss Irene sniffed. "I used to be a perfect size ten all during my twenties, just like you."

"I'm a size twelve, Mommy." Faith smiled. "That means you were smaller than me."

"Mm hmm, I probably was," Miss Irene said as she took a sip of her wine. "And I was just as pretty as you, too, and my hair was thick and long, and all down my back." Miss Irene sat up straight as she remembered her youth, her eyes taking on a faraway look. "That's when all the men were chasing me. All I had to do was go like this," Miss Irene gave an impetuous snap of her fingers, "and some man would be at my side, asking what he could do to make me happy."

"I know, Mommy. I love to look at your old pictures. I've never seen anyone as beautiful." Faith grinned, happy that her mother had broken out of despair, if only temporarily. "Aunt Gloria always said all the boys on the block used to hang around your building, waiting for you to come out so they could walk you to school."

"They sure did." Miss Irene grinned, the faraway look still in her eyes. "All the other girls used to be so jealous, even your Aunt Gloria. And you know how they say the prettiest girls used to end up without dates on Saturday night because boys were afraid to ask them out? Bunch of lies." Miss Irene started laughing. "I used to go to the early movie with one guy, have him get me back home just in time for me to change my clothes and go to the Apollo Theater with another guy, get rid of him, and then go sit out the steps with another guy just talking all night until my daddy made me come inside.

"Oh, I was 'Miss It' back in those days. Folks used to compare me to Diahann Carroll—of course I was much lighter than her and had freckles." Miss Irene giggled. "That's what drew me to your father, Faith. He's the only person I know besides me that looked downright gorgeous with freckles. A lot of people with freckles look cute, but John and I were downright gorgeous. Everyone thought we made such a gorgeous couple. And listen, you did not hear me say a cute couple. People used to say we were a gorgeous couple—and we were."

"I know." Faith leaned down and kissed her mother on the cheek. "Hold on a minute, Mommy . . . I have to check the corn bread real quick. I'll be right back."

"Your father was crazy about me, Faith. I hope you know that. Just like Henry is about you," Miss Irene hollered after Faith. "He worshipped the ground that I walked on. Even after we were married and I started to gain all this weight because of my hypothyroidism."

Faith pulled the corn bread out of the oven and placed it on the counter top. Then she pulled her cell phone from her pants pocket while her mother continued to talk—loudly—about her more slender youth.

"Henry, where are you? I thought you'd be here by now!"

"My plane was late getting in, babe. How's the Queen Mother holding up?"

"She's still really, really upset. And it didn't help that Johnny and Allen bailed out on dinner." Faith sighed.

"You're kidding. Well, I shouldn't be more than another fifteen minutes," Henry said. "And hey, I'll stop and get some Breyers vanilla ice cream from the corner store. That might help cheer her up."

"Faith," Miss Irene continued to holler as if it were perfectly natural to have a conversation across two rooms, "remember that time your father and I took you kids to Coney Island and that guy on the D train kept winking at me, and your father got mad? I had already picked up a lot of weight by then, but I was still looking good, wasn't I? I mean, I still had men trying to pick me up in the street and all."

"And you still look good, Mommy," Faith hollered back as she gave the collard greens one last stir before removing them from the stove. The smothered chicken was done, the red rice was done, the greens were done, and the corn bread was done. They'd be able to eat as soon as Henry arrived. She looked at her watch. Seven o'clock, not too bad.

"Well, you know I always try to look good." Miss Irene was pouring another glass of wine as Faith walked back into the bedroom. "My mother always told me that a young woman should look her best when she steps out of her door. Some women just let themselves go when they get big, but not me. I've always gotten stares from men when I walk down the street."

Faith picked up the wine bottle to pour herself a glass but found, to her surprise, that it was empty. How many glasses had her mother had? she wondered.

"Faith, sweetie, is the food ready?"

"Yes, but I just spoke to Henry on the cell and he should be here within the next ten or fifteen minutes, so I figured we could just wait for him." Faith couldn't detect a slur in her mother's voice, or much of a change in her behavior, but then again, the woman always could hold her liquor. The few times that Ronald did take Miss Irene out to the bar with him, she would drink him under the table, then be able to walk out and hail them both a cab.

"Okay, but call him again and tell him to stop at the liquor store and get another bottle of Manischewitz. A large bottle, okay?"

"Sure, Mom."

"You know, I really loved Ronald," Miss Irene said in a strained voice. "And I think he really loved me, too. It was just too much drama, I think."

"That's probably it, Mommy. Some people are like that. Henry complains all the time that we're the most dramatic, hollering folks he knows." Faith started setting up the television tables that they would be eating on. "Ronald was always the quiet type. I bet we drove him nuts."

"Ronald was the only man I've ever loved since your father and Papa," Miss Irene continued. "Your father died and Papa left. And now Ronald's gone." Miss Irene started sniffling again.

"I know, Mommy, but it's going to be okay. And, you know, maybe he'll be back. He's probably just off drinking somewhere right now, thinking what a mistake he made and trying to figure out how to come back without looking bad," Faith said halfheartedly. "You know how men are."

"Yeah, I sure do," Miss Irene grunted. "He's not coming back, though."

"How do you know? He knows no one's going to treat him as good as you, always fussing over him and everything."

"I just know. It was too much drama for him." Miss Irene removed her glasses and dabbed at her eyes again, then blew her nose.

"You know," Miss Irene said suddenly, "it's really that damn Hope's fault."

Faith started chewing on her lips to keep from saying anything. She knew her mother was going to go there eventually, although she had been praying she wouldn't. She snapped the third television tray into place and then straightened up.

"I said," Miss Irene said in a louder voice, "that it's that heifer Hope's fault that Ronald left. She's the one that caused all this trouble. Ronald and I were doing quite well before she tried to seduce him."

"Whatever, Mommy. I'm going to check on the food." Faith started out of the room.

"Don't you 'whatever' me, young lady!" Miss Irene yelled after her.

"Then don't go blaming everything on Hope!" Faith whirled around to face her mother.

"You wouldn't be saying that if she was going to bed with all of your boyfriends like she does mine," Miss Irene snarled. "How can you even try to defend her?"

Faith glared at her mother, but said nothing.

"I asked you a question!" Miss Irene yelled. "How are you going to stand in my house and try to defend that little slut?"

"She's not a slut, Mommy. She's your daughter. And if she's a slut, then you made her that way." Faith said evenly.

"I made her that way? *What the hell are you talking about?*"

"Nothing!" Faith turned to walk out of the room.

"Get your ass back in here, Faith. Don't make me get up off of this bed!"

"Mommy, I'm not going to just stand here and call Hope a bunch of names," Faith yelled.

"And I'm not going to sit here and let you say it's my fault that the little slut tried to go to bed with Ronald!"

"And what makes you think he wasn't trying just as hard to go to bed with her, too!" Faith yelled. "And what makes you think they hadn't been going to bed before you caught them? And why haven't you started to think that maybe the real reason he left was because now that you put Hope out, he can't play musical beds!"

Miss Irene's mouth flew open and she stared at Faith for a few seconds. Then, without saying a word, she picked up the empty wine bottle and smashed it against the television set. Broken glass flew across the room.

"*Get out! Get out of my house right now!*" Miss Irene shouted hoarsely. "*You're just as evil as your twin! Get out of my house right now! I don't have any daughters!*"

"Oh, God. Mommy, please, I'm so sorry—" Faith began.

"Don't you say another word. Just get out of my house!" Miss Irene yelled hysterically. "You knew that bitch was sleeping with Ronald behind my back and you didn't say anything to me?"

"Mommy, no. I don't know what they were doing, or if they were doing anything." Faith started walking toward her mother slowly, her hands outstretched, as if hoping her mother would also reach out to her. "I just said that because I was mad at you for calling Hope all kinds of names."

"You're lying!" Miss Irene yelled.

"No, I'm not, Mommy." Faith continued her slow advance. "Mommy, please calm down. I'm so sorry."

"You say some shit like that to me, in my own house, and then you tell me to calm down?" Miss Irene put her hands over her face and started crying. "I sacrificed my whole life for my kids and they treat me like this?"

Faith sat down on the bed and tried to cradle her mother in her arms. "Mommy, I'm so sorry. I really am. Please don't cry."

"Faith, Faith, please, tell me, you really were lying just now, right? You really don't think Hope and Ronald were messing around in this house behind my back, do you?" Miss Irene started grabbing at Faith frantically.

"Mommy, I swear I don't," Faith said soothingly. "I really don't."

"Okay, okay. I'm sorry, I just lost it." Miss Irene sat up again and wiped her eyes. "But you can't go around saying mean things like that and not expect a reaction, you know."

"I know, Mommy. I'm really sorry." Faith sniffed, trying to fight back her own tears.

"Okay, baby. Be a good girl and clean up all this glass before Henry walks in here and thinks we've both gone loco."

"Is everything okay? I heard some glass smashing and I thought you might have fallen, Miss Irene." Faith and her mother looked up to see Tina standing over them. Oh great, just what we needed, Faith thought.

"What happened?" Tina asked as she took in the damaged television set. "Was someone fighting or something?"

"Hey, what happened in here?" Henry's voice boomed from the doorway. Faith jumped up from the bed. "You guys okay?"

"We're fine, sweetie." Miss Irene broke out in a watery smile at the sight of Henry. "Come give me a hug. And be careful not to step on any of this glass."

Henry gave Faith a quick peck on the cheek, then bent down and hugged Miss Irene.

"Look at you," Miss Irene said when he stepped back. "That's a new diamond earring in your ear, isn't it?"

"Well, you know how I just love diamonds," Henry said in an effeminate voice. He put his hand behind his head and struck a couple of profile poses in front of Miss Irene while batting his eyes. "Tell me, dearie, don't I just look divine?"

"You are so silly, Henry." Miss Irene giggled.

"Well, I'm glad you like it, Mother Irene." Henry grinned. "I've got a pair just like it for you. I've got to dig it out of my luggage, though."

"Oh, Henry," Miss Irene clapped her hands gleefully, "you treat me so good. Doesn't he treat me good, Tina?"

"Yeah, he's a good guy." Tina grinned. "Hey, what's that I smell? I know you ain't cooking, Miss Irene."

"No, my baby came over to cook me dinner," Miss Irene said happily. "Hey, why don't you stay and have dinner with us? You don't mind, do you Faith? Set up another table for Tina."

Faith obediently pulled another tray from the stack in the corner.

"Okay, let me run up to my room and turn off the stove," Tina said quickly. "I was going to cook myself some hamburgers, but whatever you guys have smells like I should be eating here."

"And let me put this ice cream in the freezer before it melts." Henry grinned and dangled a brown paper bag in front of Miss Irene. "Breyers vanilla, Mother Irene? Do I know how to treat my girl, or what?"

"Ooh, that's why I love you!" Miss Irene grinned back. "What about the wine?"

"What wine?"

"Didn't Faith call you and tell you to pick up a bottle of wine?" Miss Irene turned to Faith accusingly.

"I'm sorry, I forgot." Faith shrugged her shoulders.

"Well looky, looky. Mother Irene is trying to get her buzz on," Henry grinned. "How about I run to the liquor store and get it now, then? Manischewitz Cream White Concord, right?"

"Faith," Miss Irene said quietly when the two were alone in the room again, "would you really have told me if you did think there was something going on between Ronald and Hope?"

Faith averted her eyes. "Mommy, I already told you I don't know if anything was going on."

"But you would have told me, if you did know, right?" Miss Irene insisted.

"Mommy, please don't be mad if I say this . . ."

"If you say what?" Miss Irene's eyes narrowed into slits.

"It didn't do me any good when I told you before, did it?" Faith's eyes were downcast as she addressed her mother.

"Told me what before?"

"When I told you about Hope and Papa," Faith said in a whisper. "You didn't do anything then."

"That was different, Faith. Hope was a kid, and I couldn't throw her out."

"But Papa was a grown man and you didn't throw him out. And you made us all live in this house knowing what he did. What was the use of my telling?" Faith's eyes brimmed with tears.

"I came and I told. I told and you didn't do anything, Mommy. You let me down, and you let Hope down."

"Faith, you were too young to understand," Miss Irene said in a pleading voice as she grabbed Faith's hands. "Papa was sorry for what he did, and it wasn't his fault alone. You don't think I saw how Hope was always flirting with him from the beginning? He was weak and he fell. And it was up to me to try to keep the family together."

Faith bit her lips to keep the words from coming out. All you did, she thought dismally, was tear the family apart.

. . .

136

"Faith, the food was delicious." Henry pushed the tray away and rubbed his stomach with a sigh. "I'm going to have to pass on the ice cream. I couldn't eat another bite."

"I'm not the least surprised." Faith playfully hit him on the head. "You couldn't be satisfied with seconds, you had to go back for thirds."

"You should be glad he likes your cooking," Mother Irene said as she pushed her plate away. "You know I taught her everything she knows in the kitchen, right?"

"You taught her well. My baby can burn!" Henry grabbed Faith and planted a quick kiss on her lips.

"Aw, look at the lovebirds," Tina cooed. "Ain't that sweet."

"Umm hmm. Tina could you fix me a bowl of ice cream? Faith's been on her feet in the kitchen all day."

"It's not a problem, Mommy," Faith protested. "I'm not even tired."

"Oh sit down, girl." Tina got up. "Sure, I'll get it, Miss Irene. I'm going to get me a bowl, too, if you don't mind."

Miss Irene waited until Tina had disappeared into the kitchen and then turned to Faith with a questioning look. "I'm surprised you haven't snapped at Tina all evening. What's the matter, are you mellowing out in your old age? Or are you beginning to finally like her?"

Faith shrugged her shoulders. The truth was she was pretty much ignoring Tina because she suspected her mother of inviting her partly to inject more drama into the evening—drama in which Faith would become a participant, rather than a spectator. She was just refusing to give her mother the pleasure.

"My baby's a lover, not a fighter." Henry snuggled Faith in his arms.

"Well you should have seen her a few weeks ago when she had

the girl hemmed up in the corner, punching her all upside the head."
Miss Irene laughed.

"What?" Henry looked at Faith quizzically, but she pursed her lips
and gave a slight shake of the head, signaling him not to feed into
her mother's attempt to shake things up.

"I told her to talk to Tina about some money that was missing and
she beat the poor girl up," Miss Irene continued, trying to get a reaction. "She's just lucky I persuaded Tina not to call the police, because
they would have locked Faith up." She shot Faith an innocent look.
"Isn't that right, sweetie?"

"Hey, Henry, did Ann or Carol mention to you that they're getting married?" Faith changed the subject.

"Yeah, come to think of it, Ann did mention it. In June, right?"
Henry started playing with Faith's hair. "Aren't you supposed to be a
bridesmaid or something?"

"Am I?" Faith said. Is Ann planning on inviting everyone but
me? What the hell is going on? she wondered. "So just when did she
happen to mention it?"

"Last week, I think. Why?"

"Did she tell you not to tell me?" Faith asked irritably.

"No, why would she do that?" Henry asked.

"Don't ask me. But she told Mommy and Hope last week, and
then told them not to tell me."

"So how did you find out?" Henry asked in surprise.

"Mom slipped up and told me." Faith sucked her teeth again.
"Good thing, too. I don't know when Ann is going to get around to
mentioning it to me."

"Sounds to me like she just didn't want to include you," Miss
Irene said. "I wonder why? Have the two of you been fighting over
clients or anything?"

"No, we never fight over clients. She has her clients and I have mine, but we always give each other a percentage because we're always depending on each other for backup. It's the same as it's always been."

"Sounds to me like she wanted to surprise you." Henry shrugged his shoulders.

"Sounds to me like she didn't want to invite you," Miss Irene said again.

"But that's the thing. If she didn't want me there, why is she inviting you guys? It doesn't make sense."

"Well, it makes sense that she would invite me," Miss Irene said huffily. "Ann thinks of me as her second mother."

Faith smiled to herself. Ann may have been fond of Miss Irene, bringing her gifts whenever she ever vacationed in Europe, but she certainly didn't think of her as a family member. Ann had only visited the house once, and although Little Miss Snow Queen expressed nothing about the disarray, Faith noticed that she didn't sit down during the entire twenty minute visit—no matter how many times Miss Irene insisted.

"Well, I've got to get to the bottom of this," Faith finally said. "And depending on what I find out, I might not even be in the wedding."

"Wedding? Who's getting married? Y'all two are getting married?" Tina walked in carrying two large bowls of ice cream, piled with whipped cream and hot fudge.

"These two? I wish." Miss Irene rolled her eyes. "They've been getting married since Faith was eighteen, and they haven't made it down the aisle yet. And here's Faith, thirty years old now."

"Twenty-nine," Faith admonished her mother.

"Oh yuck! Why'd you put all this crap on good ice cream?" Miss Irene drew back as Tina offered her one of the bowls.

"Crap? Oh, dang, Miss Irene. I went upstairs to my room to get these toppings. I thought I was going to surprise you," Tina said apologetically.

"You don't put toppings on good ice cream like Breyers vanilla." Miss Irene rolled her eyes. "If I wanted all that junk on it I would have asked for a store brand. You're supposed to savor good ice cream, not smother the taste with all this stuff."

"Ah, it seems you didn't know that Queen Mother was a connoisseur." Henry took the bowl that Miss Irene had rejected. "Me, personally, I don't have any taste—so I'll do you a favor and make sure this bowl doesn't go to waste."

Faith hit him on the arm. "I thought you couldn't eat another bite."

"That was a whole fifteen minutes ago, babe," Henry said as he ate a huge spoonful.

"Here I've got my mouth all ready for Breyers vanilla . . ." Miss Irene began.

"I'll get you a bowl, Mommy." Faith started to get up, but Tina waved her off.

"No, I've got it. I messed everything up, I'll get it straight," she said. "It'll just be a minute, Miss Irene."

"Oh, thank you, Tina," Faith said sweetly.

"I don't know why you're acting so nice to her all of a sudden," Miss Irene grumbled when Tina was out of earshot. "She probably did that nonsense on purpose to get me mad."

"I'm sure she didn't, Mommy," Faith answered.

"Hmmph, you don't know that girl," Miss Irene huffed. "And just so you know, she's acting all sweet to you now, but she really can't stand you. She was telling me the other day that she couldn't see how Hope and I could have a snob like you in the family."

"Ooh, listen to you, Mother Irene. Trying to start a fight," Henry said teasingly. "Mother Irene, the instigator."

"No, it's just that I don't like hypocrites. That girl's smiling all in Faith's face and she can't stand her," Miss Irene grumbled.

"Well, it's not like I care one way or the other." Faith shrugged.

"That's right, baby. Don't be letting your mama talk you into a fight." Henry gave Faith's shoulder a quick squeeze and then he turned back to Miss Irene. "I'm going to have to start calling you Donna King. Don King's younger sister."

"Stop teasing me," Miss Irene huffed. "I'm not trying to instigate anything. I just wanted to let my daughter know what's been going on behind her back. I don't think we should be keeping secrets like that between family, that's all."

"Oh, admit it, Mother Irene." Henry reached over and pinched Miss Irene's cheek. "You just want to see a little drama. Nothing wrong that. Just please don't do it at my baby's expense."

"No, I don't like drama! That's what's wrong around here. Too much drama!" To Faith and Henry's surprise, Miss Irene's eyes filled with tears. She sniffed a couple of times, then reached for another tissue. Faith quickly got up and went over to her mother.

"Mommy, come on. Everything's going to be . . ."

"Leave me alone, Faith," Miss Irene snapped. She reached for the bottle of wine that Henry had bought, already half-empty, and re-filled her glass.

"Mommy, don't you think you've had enough wine?" Faith asked gently.

"No, I don't." Miss Irene glared at Faith and took a large gulp.

"You're going to get an upset stomach drinking all that wine and having ice cream, too," Henry offered.

"I'm grown." Miss Irene took another gulp as if to prove her point. "And I don't appreciate you insinuating that I'm a drama queen, Henry. I don't deserve that." She put the glass down and dabbed at her eyes again. "I'm not used to all this drama around here.

Always drama. I don't try to make drama. I'm always the one that has to deal with it, is all."

"Hey, I didn't mean to upset you, Mother Irene. I thought you knew I was only kidding."

"I'm not upset!" Miss Irene emptied her glass then reached for the bottle. Faith gave Henry a helpless look, but said nothing. "I'm just trying to deal with everything, like always. And by myself, like always. You and Faith have each other. Hope, that heifer, has Faith. Who do I have?" She took another gulp of wine. "You know, when I was growing up, I was the baby in the family. I grew up in a big, fine apartment in Sugar Hill, did I ever tell you that, Henry? My family had so much money that my mother had hired help. We used to have a woman come in every Wednesday and Saturday and do all the washing and housework. I never had to lift a finger. And everyone loved me."

"Everyone still loves you, Mommy." Faith glanced at Henry for support.

"You know I adore you, Miss Irene," he said obligingly.

Miss Irene snorted. "You adore Faith. You tolerate me and the rest of us because of it. You don't fool me, Henry. But I adore Faith, too. And if you adore her, then I adore you." She took another gulp. "But it's not the same as you adoring me. And that's what I'm talking about."

"I adore you, Mommy," Faith said softly.

"I know you do, baby," Miss Irene reached over and touched her lightly on the hand. "You don't always say it, but you don't have to. You show me, all the time, and that's enough. But, anyway," she took another gulp of wine, "that's not what I'm talking about. I'm talking about someone really adoring and loving me. And not just my daughter." She started dabbing at her eyes again, and sniffling. "And it seems whenever I really have anyone in my life, someone always comes along and messes it up."

Faith closed her eyes and shook her head. Here we go again, she thought. I was hoping we were finished with this. She looked at Henry for help, but he said nothing.

"I know you don't like Papa because of all the things that Faith told you, but he wasn't all that bad, you know." Miss Irene sniffed. "He was my knight in shining armor. Just like you were Faith's. Papa came into my life when I really needed someone."

"Come on, Mommy, do we really need to talk about this?" Faith asked irritably.

"You can leave if you want to," Miss Irene snapped. "I was talking to Henry." She poured another glass of wine. The bottle was now almost empty.

"John Freeman died adoring me, but he adored me because of his memory of who I used to be. God knows I didn't want him to get hit by that car, but he did. And when his insurance money was used up, it was up to me to try and raise four kids the best way I could. And there weren't a whole lot of men chasing after me like they used to when I was a teenager, either. You know I used to look real good, Henry. Just like Faith."

"You still look good," Henry said gently. Miss Irene ignored him.

"So then I met Papa. He didn't care that I was a large-sized woman, and he didn't care that I had four children. He adored me. Me! And he was a good man, too. He married me and just took over the household. He was a good man and a good husband. He brought his paycheck home every week and he used to bring me flowers every Friday. And I don't care what Faith told you, he was a damn good father."

Faith involuntarily sucked her teeth.

"Stop it, Faith!" Miss Irene said. "If it wasn't for Papa you wouldn't have been able to go to all those fancy dance classes you used to love. I couldn't afford it when it was just me working. And he kept you and the kids dressed nicer than any of the children in the neighborhood, didn't he? And he tried to get close to you, but you just wouldn't let him. You were cold to him from the first time you laid eyes on him. Admit it. You never liked him. But that didn't stop him from treating you just as good as he treated the other kids. That's just the kind of man he was."

"You are so in denial!" Faith jumped over from the bed. "That man was a pervert who screwed one of your daughters and was intent on raping the other one!"

"Faith!" Henry jumped up and tried to grab her.

"No." She shook him loose and glared down at her mother. "He was a child molester, Mommy. Admit it. Say it. He was a fucking child molester who was screwing your eleven-year-old daughter!"

"She started it!" Miss Irene hollered. "You were there! You saw what she did! Always walking around in her panties in front of him!"

"She was a kid, Mommy. She was your kid!"

"She was a little slut, even then. But I was blind because of mother love. But she was born a slut. And jealous of me. Always trying to hurt me and take everything from me." Miss Irene was almost frothing at the mouth. "She went to bed with him because she was jealous of the way he adored me. Just like she goes after every other man who comes into this house!"

"Come on, baby. Calm down, this isn't helping." Henry tried to pull Faith into his arms, but she resisted.

"She didn't go to bed with him!" Faith yelled at her mother. "He raped her. She was only eleven. He raped her. He was a pervert. A child molester. You brought a child molester into our house. Our family. It wasn't Hope's fault and you know it. It's your fault! You let that dirty bastard screw your baby daughter and you didn't do anything to stop him. Even when you knew! Even when I told!"

Miss Irene jumped off the bed and threw a fist at her daughter, but Henry swung Faith out of the way just in time and the punch landed on his shoulder, almost tumbling him backward.

"You tell me you love me and then you say all this shit to me." Miss Irene tried to reach behind Henry. "Let go of her!"

"Let go of me, Henry," Faith shouted as he tried with one hand to hold her back, and with the other to fend off Miss Irene's blows. "Let her hit me. That's just what she always does. Lashes out at the wrong person. Why are you mad at me, Mommy? Because I'm telling what you did? Or because I told you in the first place, huh? Is that what this is, Mommy? Because I told you what Papa was doing to Hope? Because I told you your man was screwing your daughter? Let go of me, Henry. Come on, Mommy. Come on, hit me!"

It was at that moment that Tina came back into the room, holding a bowl of ice cream, and to everyone's astonishment, Hope was behind her.

"What the hell is going on?" was all Hope managed to get out before Miss Irene ran over and landed a punch on her chin, knocking her into the wall. She then grabbed Hope by the throat and started punching and clawing at her.

"*Get off her!*" Faith broke loose from Henry and hurled herself between Hope and her mother. Hope then sunk to the floor, gasping for air. Faith threw herself on top of her sister and took Miss Irene's kicks and punches.

"Stop it! All of you just stop it." Henry grabbed Miss Irene by her arms and tried unsuccessfully to pin them behind her back. "Don't just stand there! Help for crying out loud," he yelled to Tina, who still stood in the doorway holding the ice cream, her mouth agape.

"Let go of me," said Miss Irene as Henry propelled her backward toward the bed. "I'm going to kill that heifer!"

"Why you want to kill her!" Faith scrambled to her feet, while Hope lay on the floor in fetal position, sobbing. "She didn't do anything. Why didn't you attack Papa, huh? Why didn't you attack him? Why didn't you throw him out of your house!"

"Faith, baby, please!" Henry was still trying to wrestle with Miss Irene, who was huffing and puffing as she tried to get back off the bed.

"Faith, what the hell is going on?" Tina tried to grab Faith with one hand while still holding the ice cream with the other.

"Ask her what's going on!" Faith yanked away. "Ask her what's been going on in this house for years!"

"Don't you dare air our laundry in front of strangers!" Miss Irene howled.

"That's right. Don't air the dirty laundry. Don't mention what happened. It's family business!" Faith yelled back as she advanced toward her mother. "You don't care what happens. You just care if someone tells, right? You just don't want me to tell. Just like you didn't want me to tell then, right? You *knew* what was going on, didn't you! Just like I knew. You knew. You just didn't want anyone to tell. Well, I told, Mommy. And I'm telling now."

"You little bitch!" Miss Irene sobbed before collapsing on the bed.

"Go on, Mommy! Tell me I'm wrong!" Faith shouted over her. "Tell me you didn't know or you didn't at least suspect! Tell me!"

"Dammit, Faith! Shut up!" Henry grabbed Faith and started pulling her toward the door.

"You just didn't want me to tell, did you, Mommy? Well, I told. I told and I'm glad I told." Faith continued to yell even as she was halfway out the door. By this time Hope had crawled across the floor and onto the bed with Miss Irene. She was trying to cradle her mother, who was sobbing uncontrollably.

"Please don't cry, Mommy," she whimpered through her own tears. "Faith, please leave her alone. Please, just stop it!"

"Let her cry! That's all she did the night I told her!" Faith yelled hysterically. She grabbed Henry's face and forced him to look her in the eyes. "Did I tell you that's all she did when I told her? She cried and then baked that sick bastard a birthday cake." Faith started crying, too, and collapsed in Henry's arms. "And she never even talked to Hope about it! She's hated her own daughter all these years, and never had the guts to even talk to her about it. All she does is lash out at her. She's our mother! Why couldn't she even sit Hope down and talk to her?"

"I know, baby," Henry said gently.

"I did what I was supposed to do, didn't I? I was supposed to tell, wasn't I?" Faith sobbed gently into Henry's shoulder.

"Yes, baby, you did the right thing."

Faith pulled away from Henry and looked over at her mother and sister who were holding each other on the bed. "Baby," she asked dismally as Henry led her out the door, "if I did the right thing, why am I crying? Why is everyone crying?"

10

I don't know. I think you're going to have to try a size five . . . that seven is sagging a little in the butt." Faith stroked her chin as Hope whirled in front of her.

"Sagging in the butt? As big as my butt is?" Hope tried to look over her shoulder to get a peek at her posterior.

"As big as your butt used to be. You've got to eat if you want to maintain your booty, Baby Girl." Faith shrugged and handed Hope the same pants in a smaller size. "Try these on while I go look for a size five in the other ones."

"Yuck! Gray flannel? I ain't wearing no gray flannel pants. You've gotta be joking!" Hope held her nose as she handed the pants back to Faith. "Besides, I ain't working for no law firm or nothing. This is for a cruise line, remember?"

"Look, Baby Girl, right now you're not working for anyone. I'm just saying this would be appropriate for the interview. Then, if you get the job, you can start dressing more casually. It's not like I'm trying to stuff you into a business suit or something."

"What do you mean 'if' I get the job. You know darn well I'ma get that job. Have I ever been turned down for a job? Puleeze." Hope laughed.

"Yeah, you get plenty of jobs. Damn shame. You can type 120 words per minute, take shorthand, and use a Dictaphone, and people just throw jobs at you when you turn on your charm at interviews. And then you turn around and quit in three months," Faith said. "You know it doesn't make sense. Here you are, twenty-nine years old, and never kept a job for a year."

Hope shrugged her shoulders. "I get bored."

"Well, just do me a favor, keep this job a year. Please? You know if you're there a year, you and a guest can get a free cruise. And I'm just dying to get on a luxury boat," Faith grumbled.

Faith looked at her watch—1:15 P.M. They had been shopping now for two hours and they had purchased only two outfits for Hope. They had shopped the day before and had found only one outfit that Hope liked, and she was wearing it now, much to Faith's dismay. Still, it would all be worth it if Hope actually landed the job. The interview was set for the next morning at eight, and since Hope was still staying with her, Faith would make sure she got there on time and properly dressed. Even if it was going to put a dent on her credit card bill and her nerves.

"Ooh, Faith, look at this!"

Faith turned to see Hope holding up a black leather miniskirt.

"Yeah, right. You're not interviewing for that line of work." Faith couldn't help but grin.

"Yeah, yeah, I know. But ya know I could do this skirt to death." Hope held the skirt up against her skinny hips. "Can't you just imagine me wearing this and some spike heels and stuff? I'd be the shit. Come on Faith, buy this for me and I promise I'll pay you back with my first paycheck."

"How much does it cost?"

Hope looked at the price tag, then suddenly flung the skirt across the department store floor, hollering, "Holy shit!"

"Hope, what the hell is wrong with you?" Faith scurried over and picked up the skirt, giving the saleswoman a weak smile of apology as she did so.

"They want $260 for that shit. Fuck. What did they do? Skin a sacred cow from India or something? They gotta be outta their fucking minds. I ain't paying that kinda money for some stupid skirt. Shit!"

"Hope! Keep your voice down. Dang, I can't take you anywhere." Faith grabbed Hope's arm and started pushing her toward the nearest exit.

"Hold up! Hold up! I gotta get this dress off and get my clothes back on else they're gonna try and arrest us and stuff." Hope struggled free of Faith's grasp. "I'm sorry, Baby Girl, but damn . . . $260 for a skirt? You know they're crazy."

Hope strutted back into the fitting room while Faith smiled at the saleswoman again. The heavily perfumed woman rolled her eyes before walking away to whisper something to the cashier. The two women looked in Faith's direction, then the cashier picked up the white telephone receiver by the cash register.

"Would someone from security please report to the juniors section," her voice trumpeted over the store intercom. Faith tapped on the fitting room door.

"Would you please hurry up so we can get out of here?" she pleaded.

"I'm coming right now. What's the matter?" Hope strolled out of the fitting room, oblivious to the drama she had just created. "You ready to roll or you wanna do some more shopping and stuff?"

"Let's get out of here." Faith grabbed her sister's arm and turned toward the exit again, but the path was blocked by a big, burly man who smelled of pipe tobacco.

"May I help you ladies with something?" he asked, eying them up and down.

"No, thank you. We were just leaving," Hope said smoothly. "This store's a little too rich for our blood." She flashed a big smile at the man.

The man gave a little grin in return. "It is rather expensive. I just wanted to make sure everything was all right."

"Oh, everything's fine!" Hope flashed an even brighter smile at the man and batted her eyelashes. "But you know, brother, you could have warned us when we came in your store that we were in for a shock when we looked at the price tags."

The man gave Hope a sheepish grin.

Another sucker under Hope's spell, Faith thought to herself. How the hell does she do that?

"And can you imagine?" Hope gave a deep sigh. "That saleswoman started acting as if we were common thieves, simply because we exclaimed about the price of an item. It's a shame the way they treat our people, isn't it?"

"I'm sure they were just trying to do their jobs, Ma'am," the man said gallantly.

"If you say so." Hope sighed again, leaning her head to the side and blinking up at the man from the best vantage point of her almond eyes.

Boy, is she laying it on thick, Faith thought.

"Well, I'll just escort you young ladies to the door then, if you don't mind," the man said with a grin.

"Not at all! And if you weren't wearing that wedding band I'd slip you my telephone number when we got there." Hope giggled and tucked her hand under the man's arm as they walked to the door with Faith following two steps behind them.

Uh oh, she's up to something. I'm going to just die if the security alarm goes off when we walk out that door. No, first I'm going to kick Hope's ass, then I'm going to die. I know she's not stupid enough to have boosted something from this store. But she's acting too nice. She's definitely up to something. Oh God, please don't let any alarms go off.

"So do you want to frisk me or something before I walk out?" Hope stepped back from the man and held her arms up at her sides, still smiling.

"Please, Ma'am. I'm not accusing you of anything," the man said with obvious embarrassment.

"Of course you aren't." Hope smiled and stepped close to the man, then snapped open her shoulder bag. "But you'd better at least look in my purse so your boss doesn't get on you."

"Ma'am . . ." the man began nervously.

"Oh come on, baby . . . I'm just playing." Hope lightly tapped the man on his chest. "In fact, I'll stop by later, and if that wedding band is in your pocket instead of on your finger, maybe I can slip you that telephone number after all? Hmm?"

"Hope! Behave yourself!" Faith said irritably.

"He knows I'm just playing!" Hope gave the man a wink, then headed out the door. Faith held her breath, praying that no light would start flashing or bells would start ringing. Her prayers were answered.

"Come on, Baby Girl! Let's go grab something to eat. I'm starved." Hope waved at her impatiently. Faith hurried out of the store, then looked back at the man, who stood there grinning and twiddling his fingers good-bye. What an idiot, she thought.

"Dang, Baby Girl, you had me worried," she said aloud as she and Hope strolled down 34th Street.

"Why?" Hope asked nonchalantly.

"I just knew you had taken something from the store, especially when you were so nice to that security guard. What was that all about?"

"Nuttin'."

"Uh huh, it was about something. I noticed your grammar improved dramatically. A sure sign that you were up to some kinda con," Faith said suspiciously.

Hope started giggling.

"Hope!" Faith stopped in her tracks and grabbed Hope by the arm, wheeling her around. "What did you do?"

"Nuttin'!" Hope jerked her arm away. "Let's go back uptown, okay?"

"I thought you wanted to stop and get something to eat?"

"Yeah, but we can just grab some takeout and eat it at the house," Hope whined.

"Nope. I'm tired and hungry. We're stopping right here." Faith looked around and noticed they were right in front of a seafood restaurant. "And right now."

"And anyway, I promised Mrs. Trumble I was gonna stop by the hospital again—"

"Visiting hours don't end until eight," Faith snapped. "Come on."

Hope sighed, but obediently followed Faith into the restaurant. As soon as the hostess seated them at a corner booth, Hope disappeared into the bathroom, leaving her sister to study the menu alone.

After she decided on a shrimp basket, Faith glanced around at the paintings on the wall. All of them were seascapes, and not her taste. She took a sip of her water and sighed, wishing Hope would hurry up so the waiter could take their order, when she heard a young woman giggling a few booths behind hers.

"Jason, stop. Someone's going to see us. Keep your hands above the table." The woman laughed.

"Hush up, girl. No one's paying us any mind," a man's voice answered.

They must be young lovers, Faith thought with a smile. She suddenly had an urge to call Henry, to tell him she missed him. He would be flying home from Chicago that night, but she was sure he would appreciate the call—especially since they'd had that big fight right before he left town. She rifled through her purse for her cell phone, but realized she had left it home. She stood up and glanced around the restaurant again, now looking for a telephone booth. In doing so, she got a look at the lusty couple and almost dropped her purse.

"Jason Fleming?" she said almost in a whisper. "I just know that's not Jason Fleming."

She quickly sat down, hoping he hadn't seen her. I've got to be wrong. I just know that Jason wouldn't be cheating on Susan already. They've been married for only three months. She pulled out her compact mirror and angled it to get a good look at the man. There was no doubt about it, she decided—it was definitely Jason sitting there, playing footsie with some chick who couldn't have been more than eighteen. She realized it seemed ridiculous, but she felt his adultery was also a betrayal against her. After all, she had been Susan's maid of honor and they had known each other since the third grade. And since Jason was new in town and didn't know anyone, Henry had been pressed into service as the best man. Just wait until she told him about Jason's infidelity. And Hope was going to be furious. She and Susan had been best friends when they were younger. The only reason Faith was Susan's maid of honor was because Hope was off on a crack binge somewhere and couldn't be found.

Oh, dang, she thought, just wait until I tell Susan. This is going to kill her. Or maybe kill him, on second thought, because Susan doesn't play. She had once seen her old schoolmate chase a man down the street with an ice pick when he tried to snatch her pocket-book. Of course, this might be different since it was her man. Some women just won't believe it when they're told that their man is cheating on them. Well, Faith decided, it was just a chance she was going to have to take. Better to lose a friendship for telling than to let her girlfriend be played for a fool. *I would certainly want to know if someone saw Henry cheating on me,* she thought.

"What's up, Baby Girl? You look like you just saw a ghost!" Hope slid into the booth, grinning like a Cheshire cat.

"Girl, you're not going to believe this—"

"Excuse me, Miss. Did you leave these in the bathroom?" A waitress was holding what appeared to be a large pair of tweezers in her hand.

"Um, yeah. Thanks." Hope took the contraption and quickly slipped it into her pocketbook.

"What was that?" Hope asked when the waitress walked away.

"Nuttin'." Hope picked up the menu and was suddenly engrossed in its contents.

"Nothing, huh?" Faith asked suspiciously. "So what would I find if I grabbed your pocketbook and looked inside?"

Hope shifted in her seat uncomfortably, but said nothing. Faith lunged across the table for the pocketbook, but Hope was quicker. She put it on the seat beside her and out of Faith's reach.

"Hope . . ." Faith said threateningly.

"Okay, look. I lifted a dress from the store and stuff. Don't make a big deal out of it, okay?" Hope picked up the menu again, but Faith grabbed it from her hands.

"You did what?" Faith said through clenched teeth. "You actually stole a dress while shopping with me? What if you had gotten caught? We'd both end up in jail. That is so fucked up, Hope."

"There wasn't any way we was gonna get caught," Hope whined.

"You was with me and you ain't even know. How was I gonna get caught, huh?"

"What about the plastic security tags they put on the clothes? What if it had set off an alarm? What then, smart-ass?" Faith hissed.

"That's what the tweezers are for. They're specially made to take off the security tags. I got it off this guy in the street for ten bucks, and I've used them before. I took the tag off in the dressing room. I musta taken the tweezers out when I was rummaging through my pocketbook while I was in the bathroom," Hope said in a reassuring voice. She reached over and put a hand over her sister's. "I wouldn'ta done it if I wasn't sure I wouldn't get caught. I ain't gonna take no stupid chances and get you in trouble."

"Ooh, you make me so mad!" Faith leaned back in her seat, smoldering. "Hey," she said suddenly, "how did you get the dress out the store? It couldn't have been in your pocketbook, because you opened it up for that security guy."

"I stuck it in my panties."

"What? Eeww!" Faith recoiled.

"Oh please. It's not like I didn't take a bath this morning." Hope giggled.

Faith sighed as she tried to decide, for the millionth time, whether Hope was simply stupid or just plain crazy. She settled, for the millionth time, on both.

"Hey, doesn't that look like Jason over there?" Hope squinted her eyes and pointed toward the booth where the adulterer sat. "Yo, Faith, that damn sure does look like Jason, doesn't it? Oh shit, that better not be Jason kissing on some girl! *Oh fuck! That is Jason!*"

Before Faith could say anything, Hope was out of her seat and flying toward the booth.

"Ooh, Jason, you are such a fucking bastard!" Hope stood in front of the couple, blocking their way out of the booth. "You ain't even married a year yet and you're out here hoing around? Oooh, I'm telling. I'm telling, I'm telling!"

A waiter spun around so fast to see what was happening that he spilled several drinks onto the floor. Restaurant patrons were standing up, trying to get a firsthand look at the commotion. Faith rushed over to stand next to her sister. The trapped girl's eyes were opened so wide she looked like an owl, and Jason was sputtering unintelligibly.

"And with a stank looking ho, too!" Hope hooted. "Damn, you oughtta be ashamed of yourself, Jason. The bitch doesn't look like she's outta diapers yet! And all emancipated and shit!"

Faith tapped her sister on the shoulder. "You mean emaciated," she said when Hope turned around.

"Yeah, emaciated." Hope swung back around and leaned across Jason to put her finger in the cowering girl's face. "That means skinny, in case you didn't know, you stupid bitch. And don't try and tell me you didn't know this motherfucker was married. I can look at your face and tell you knew, you stank bitch. Don't you think she knew?" Hope turned to her twin.

"Yeah, she probably did. It's not like he isn't wearing his wedding band," Faith said in a solemn tone while struggling not to let her laughter burst through. "And if she didn't know, he certainly did."

"Yeah, you're the one who took the wedding vows, you lying bastard." Hope started jabbing Jason in the chest. "You lied to God and to Susan. Just wait till I get uptown and tell her I saw you in here kissing on some bitch."

"Naw, naw, this is my cousin," a terrified Jason finally managed to get out. "Naw, you got it all wrong, this is my cousin!"

"Cousin my ass!" Hope hollered. "What ya'll supposed to be, kissing cousins or something? Well, y'all can kiss my ass because I'm telling Susan! As God is my witness I'm going to tell on your stank cheating ass!"

The girl, who was seated closest to the wall, was blubbering un-controllably. Jason tried to slide out of the booth, but Hope moved in even closer, expertly blocking him in.

"Oh, you just gonna push me, motherfucker? What, you're an adulterer and a woman beater, too?" she hollered at the top of her lungs.

"I ain't touch you!" Jason turned to Faith with a pleading look in his eyes. "I ain't touch her."

"It looked like you touched her to me, and you'd better not do it again or both me and my sister will kick your funky ass," Faith hissed at him.

"That's right! And then my brother-in-law will kick your ass, too! I oughtta call him right now! Naw, fuck that, I'm gonna go call Su-san!" Hope looked around for her pocketbook and, realizing that it was still in their abandoned booth, turned back to Jason. "Yo, moth-erfucker, gimme a quarter so I can go call your wife!"

"Excuse me, Miss, but we're going to have to ask you to leave. You're disturbing the other patrons," the nervous restaurant manager told Hope.

"Pardon me, but I'm in the middle of a situation here." Hope held her hand up in front of the manager's face. "Do you mind?"

"Miss, I'm sorry, but I really have to ask that you leave." The waiter tried to grab Hope's arm.

"Take your hands off my sister!" Faith roared as she stepped to-ward the manager, causing the startled man to stumble back.

"Well, I'm just going to have to call the police," he finally said.

"You do that, but don't you lay another hand on my sister or I'll have you arrested for assault. You got that?"

Instead of replying, the manager turned around and shouted to the hostess, "Marcia, call the police. *Now!*"

"I'm glad he's calling the police. I'm gonna make them arrest you for adultery!" Hope returned her attention to Jason, who looked like he was going to start crying any minute. "I'm going to make sure they lock your ass up for cheating on a nice girl like Susan." She paused, and then turned to Faith. "Adultery is illegal, isn't it?"

"Umm, I don't know if it's illegal in New York City. I mean, if it was, they'd even have to lock the mayor up. But it is immoral," Faith offered.

"Good, then I'm gonna call the fucking Pope on your immoral fucking ass!" Hope swung around and put her finger in Jason's face again. "Naw, first I'm gonna call Susan. 'Cause I'm telling on you, bitch. I'm telling. And where's that quarter I asked you for?" Hope hollered at Jason. "An adulterer, a woman beater, and a cheap motherfucker to boot. You are some fucking prize!"

‖

The heat in the apartment was unbearable. Faith used a damp washcloth to wipe the sweat from her forehead and looked at the clock on the living room wall. Nine o'clock. She had called the superintendent more than an hour ago to complain. The boiler was out of whack, he told her. The thermostat was broken and the shut-off valve was stuck. He assured Faith that he had called in for an emergency repairman. He obviously had not yet arrived, because apartment 2A, and every other apartment in the building, had been converted into a spacious sauna. The radiators hissed furiously as they released their steam, and pools of water began to form around their bases on the floor.

"I can't believe we're sitting here in the middle of December, stripped down to our bras and panties and drinking ice-cold lemonade." She let her head loll back on the luxurious white sofa, then shifted her head to the right and looked at her sister laying face-down and spread-eagled on the hardwood floor. "Well, me sitting and you positioned for kinky sex."

"The sofa and chairs are too hot," Hope said wearily, not raising her head from the floor. "And it's cooler down here. You should try it."

"No thanks." Faith reached for the remote control and switched the channel from Nickelodeon to AMC, which was showing *Young Guns*. "Hey." She looked at Hope again. "Who do you think is sexier? Charlie Sheen or Emilio Estevez?"

"Emilio Estevez," Hope said, her voice partially muffled by the floor.

"Yeah, me too." Faith switched to another station, which was showing *Vampire in Brooklyn*.

"Eddie Murphy or Kadeem Hardison?" she asked.

"Eddie Murphy," came the muffled reply.

"I kind of like Kadeem better. He has an innocent quality about him. Eddie Murphy always looks like he's up to something." Faith picked up her sweaty glass of lemonade from the white fiberglass end table and took a long sip.

"Aw, Faith. Why don'tcha change the channel? We already done watched one scary movie tonight." Hope looked up from the floor. "You know I get nightmares."

"Maybe we should put some clothes on and go back out on the fire escape?" Faith switched to the Home Shopping Network. "Nah, never mind, it's too cold out there."

"Too cold out there and too damn hot in here," Hope grumbled as her head lolled back onto the floor.

"Yeah, this would be the one winter night when there's no wind. We're not even getting a breeze through the windows." Faith sighed. Normally she would have spent the night over at her mother's house to escape the heating problem in her apartment, especially since Henry had called at 5:00 P.M. to say his flight out of Chicago's O'Hare airport had been canceled because of bad weather. But she hadn't spoken to her mother since the scene the week before. Hope had seen Tina in the street afterward and was told that Miss Irene said she never wanted to see either of them ever again. Still, they couldn't very well stay in the apartment in this heat; it would be impossible to sleep, and Hope had that job interview in the morning.

"Should we go to a hotel?" she asked Hope.

"You paying?"

"Yeah."

"What hotel?"

"You can pick."

"The Waldorf-Astoria?" Hope looked up from the floor hopefully.

"You want me to spend five hundred dollars to shack up with you?" Faith sucked her teeth. "Go to hell."

"I've been there for the last two hours," Hope groaned, then let her head fall to the floor, a little more forcefully than she intended. "Ouch!"

"Hey!" Faith threw down the magazine she had been using to fan herself. "Listen to that!"

"Listen to what?" Hope crawled to her knees while rubbing her forehead.

"The hissing stopped. The guy must have come and fixed the boiler!" Faith said excitedly. She jumped up, suddenly filled with energy, and ran to touch the radiator. It was still hot, but the hissing had definitely ceased.

"Maybe it was my head hitting the floor," Hope giggled excitedly. "I think I should get the credit. And the pay, too."

"Whatever! Let's get ready for bed, Baby Girl. You have to be up early to make that interview." Faith hummed happily as she tidied up the living room.

"Yeah, I am sleepy." Hope got up from the floor and stretched. "Can I sleep with you since Henry ain't gonna be coming in tonight?"

Faith laughed. "Hope, you're such a baby. I bet that's the real reason you're always picking at Henry—because he sleeps with me so you can't."

"I pick at him because he picks at me." Hope shrugged. "And I told you I ain't wanna watch that scary movie before. Now you gotta let me sleep with you."

Faith gulped down the last of her lemonade. "Yeah, all right. But don't be holding my feet like you used to when you were scared. You're too grown for all that."

"Whatever." Hope headed for the bedroom.

It was cold. In fact, it was freezing. Faith tried to move closer to the edge of the bed so that she could check the alarm clock, but found to her horror that she could not move her legs. Her mind flew back to the Alfred Hitchcock film she and Hope had watched on television, about a paralyzed man who was nearly embalmed because he could not tell anyone he was alive. But she could move her arm, couldn't she? Yes, she could. She was too terrified to try and move her head. What if she couldn't? She wanted to call out to Hope, but what if no voice came out? Wait a minute . . . Hope. Where was Hope? Had the force that was now holding her legs in a paralyzing grip earlier squeezed the breath from her beloved twin? Faith's eyes flew open in terror. She opened her mouth to scream, but just then a foot landed unceremoniously, and very painfully, on her nose.

"Damn it, Hope, you kicked me!" Faith tried unsuccessfully to sit up in the bed. "And let go of my feet!"

"Huh? What?" Hope said sleepily from under the covers.

"Let go of my feet!" Faith tried to squirm her legs out of Hope's grasp, but her twin's grip was too tight. "*Let go!*"

"Yeah, yeah, stop yelling and stuff!" Hope sat up at the foot of the bed and started rubbing her eyes. "What time is it? God, it's freezing in here."

"I know. I was *trying* to get up and grab another blanket for the bed, but I couldn't get up, because *you* were holding onto my legs for dear life. I hate it when you do that!" Faith flounced out of the bed and grabbed a beige wool blanket from the top shelf of the bedroom closet. "You act like I'm your personal security blanket."

"Baby Girl, please, you should be used to it by now. I've done that all our lives," Hope yawned, then climbed back under the sheet and comforter. "And anyway, it's your fault. You were the one that wanted to watch scary movies."

"*No!* You're sleeping in the guest room." Faith snatched the covers off of her sister.

"Faith, stop, it's freezing in here!" Hope grabbed frantically for the covers.

"You promised you weren't going to hold onto my feet!" Faith snapped.

"I'm sorry, okay? I won't do it again and stuff," Hope snapped back. "And why is it so cold in here?"

"I guess fixing the heat must have meant turning it off. Get up and let me spread the comforter and blanket over the bed," Faith grumbled.

They were back in bed in less than five minutes, but Faith was wide awake. She glanced over at the alarm clock: 1:30 A.M. She could still get five hours of rest if she fell asleep immediately. She closed her eyes, then opened them a few seconds later. No use faking it, she just wasn't sleepy. At least Hope wasn't still clinging to her legs.

"Hey, Baby Girl . . . remember when we all used to crawl up in Mommy's bed when the heat was turned off 'cause we couldn't pay the gas bill? Me, you, Johnny, and Allen?" Hope's voice came from the foot of the mattress.

"Yeah, and we would argue over who was going to sleep next to Johnny because he would always pee in the bed." Faith giggled.

"Yeah, and I always lost the argument. You so mean." Hope giggled back. "But those were the days, weren't they? I mean, we ain't had no money, but it was still kinda nice and stuff. The whole family was real close then, weren't we?"

"Yeah, before Mommy hooked up with Papa and he ruined everything." Faith closed her eyes again, knowing the conversation was over. It always was when she brought up Papa's name. The room was silent, as she knew it would be, and she started drifting back off to sleep.

"He wasn't all that bad."

Faith opened her eyes. "Huh?"

"I was just saying he wasn't all that bad," Hope repeated softly.

"Please. He was despicable," Faith snapped. "Look at what he did to you. He was a pervert. A damn pedophile. And I hope he rots in hell." Faith started chewing on her bottom lip, trying to keep back the rest of the venom boiling inside of her. She knew how much it bothered Hope when she spoke badly about Papa, but she hated him so much. Yet at the same time, she didn't want to shut down the conversation. She waited, praying Hope would say something else.

"But you know, it really wasn't all his fault." Hope was speaking so softly Faith could barely hear her. "It ain't like he raped me. I mean, it may have been statutory rape, 'cause I was underage and stuff, but he ain't hold me down and force me to do anything. I don't think he even started the whole thing. In fact, I know he didn't. I did."

Faith said nothing, hoping that her sister would continue. It had been almost twenty years, and Hope had never talked about her relationship with Papa. Why is she doing it now? Faith wondered. Maybe because it was dark and they were on different ends of the bed so Hope didn't have to look at her while she talked. Faith was afraid to move, to even shift in the bed, because doing so might cause this important moment to pass.

"All these years you've been hating Papa because of what he did, but it was really my fault." There were tears in Hope's voice, and Faith wanted to comfort her sister, but sensed that it would be wrong to do so. Hope had to get this out of her system, finally.

"Y'all were at the swimming pool, and I stayed home with Papa and was watching television, and we was hugging up when some mushy movie came on. And when the girl kissed the guy, I kissed Papa. On the mouth. And he kissed me back. And that's how the whole thing started. See? It was my fault, not his." Hope broke out in soft sobs, but Faith didn't move. As much as it pained her to hear her sister cry, she knew this scene had to be finished.

"See? All this time you been hating Papa for hurting me and Mommy, but it was really all my fault. I am the one who started it. I'm the one that hurt Mommy. I was such a bitch. How could I have done that to my own mother?" Hope was sobbing incessantly now, and Faith could restrain herself no longer. She burrowed under the covers to the foot of the bed and grabbed her sister in a bear hug, but, to her surprise, Hope wiggled away and turned her back to her, burying her head in her hands as she continued to cry. Not knowing what else to do, Faith grabbed her sister from behind.

"Hope, honey, don't you see! It's not your fault! He was a grown man and he knew what he was doing. You were only eleven," Faith said soothingly.

"Ten," Hope sobbed.

"Huh?"

"I was ten. You ain't catch us until I was eleven." Hope sobbed harder.

"That's even worse. Come on, you were a kid." Faith threw the covers off of them and forced her sister into a sitting position. Hope still wouldn't face her, though, so Faith rubbed her sister's back and shoulders as she talked and Hope cried.

"There's a reason that it's illegal to have sex with kids under a certain age. At ten years old you're still playing double-dutch and hide-and-go-seek. You're still doing stupid things like chasing balls in the street without looking to see if there's a car coming," Faith said soothingly. "You don't have enough reasoning power to decide to have sex when you're ten. You were a child and he was an adult. He was your parent, for God's sake. It was his responsibility to look out for you, not to take advantage of you. But he was a pedophile. He knew what he was doing. You may have thought it was your idea to kiss him, but he was buttering you up to get to that point. It was all part of his plan . . ." Hope suddenly reared up, throwing Faith backward on the bed.

"Stop it!" Hope jumped up from the bed, turned around, and glared at her sister through teary eyes. "I'm trying to take responsibility for what I did and you're busy blaming someone else. I was the one that was wrong. Me! I came on to him. I seduced my own stepfather!"

Faith scrambled out of bed, pulling blankets to the floor, and tried to rush to her sister, but Hope backed away.

"Hope, listen to yourself," Faith pleaded. "I don't have a problem with someone taking responsibility for their own actions, but are you even listening to what you're saying? *How can a ten-year-old seduce a grown man?*"

"But I . . . I . . ." Hope stumbled backward and bumped into the dresser. A bottle of perfume tumbled over, its loose top releasing the scent of Shalimar onto the carpet. Hope stared down at the floor and started wailing, as if wounded. She backed up again, until she hit the wall and could go no further.

"*Baby girl, you were a victim!* He was a predator and you were his prey. And he tore you up. He tore all of us up." Faith started toward her sister again, but then doubled over and started crying.

"And you've been punishing yourself ever since!" She looked up at Hope and screamed. "Why are you doing this to yourself? *Why are you doing this to me!*"

"*I'm not doing anything to you! You just don't understand . . .*"

"*No! You don't understand. You're killing me!*" Faith hollered through her tears. "*I'm watching you kill yourself smoking crack and selling your body to any man with five dollars, and it's fucking killing me!*" Tears streamed down her face as she sank to her knees. "You're killing yourself, Baby Girl. And I know it's my fault, and it's killing me. It's fucking killing me."

Hope hurried to hug her sister, who was crying so hard she was near convulsions. "Shh . . . shh . . . it's not your fault. How can it be your fault?"

"I don't know, but I know it is!" Faith wailed. "I'm supposed to protect you and look out for you, and you're killing yourself and there's nothing I can do."

Her head lolled back and would have hit the floor if Hope had not been holding her so tightly. "Oh, Hope, I really hate Papa," she wailed.

"Me too, Baby Girl," Hope sobbed softly as she rocked back and forth with her twin in her arms. "Me too."

Faith tried to wipe the tears from her face, but gave up since more were still pouring from her eyes. She buried her face in Hope's shoulder and continued to sob.

"Shh . . . It's all right, Sis. It's okay," Hope cooed in a teary voice.

The irony suddenly hit Faith. Hadn't it started out with her trying to console Hope? How did their roles get reversed? Wasn't she the one who always supplied the comfort?

Faith lifted her head from her sister's shoulder and cupped her hands around Hope's face so she could look directly in her eyes. "Hope, you've got to get help. You can't go on like this." She sniffed back the tears as she spoke.

"Faith. I don't know." Hope tried, unsuccessfully, to push her sister's hands away.

"Hope, please . . . for me. I don't ask you for much," Faith said frantically. "Just do this one thing for me. Maybe you can go to a rehab center, one with some doctors you can talk to, and get to the real root of your problems."

"But we know the root of my problems already, don't we? We just agreed it's what happened with Papa," Hope said dismally. "So now that we've talked about it, why do I need to go see someone, Baby Girl?"

"Hope, please!" Faith let go of Hope's face and buried her own in her hands—her back heaving with sobs.

"Faith, no . . . I'm gonna go see someone, I promise." Hope started rubbing Faith's back. "I'll try and find someone tomorrow if you want, okay? I promise. Just stop crying and let's get back into bed so we can get some sleep.

"Hey, I have to get up in a couple of hours to make that job interview, remember? Come on and let's get back in bed so I can get my beauty rest," Hope said jokingly.

Faith jumped up as if she'd been shot. "Oh, God, I forgot. Oh, Hope, I'm so sorry."

"That's okay." Hope got up from the floor and stretched. "But let's see if we can get at least a couple of hours sleep, okay? I'm sleepy as all hell.

"Good night, Baby Girl," Hope said softly after they both climbed back into the bed.

"Good night, Baby Girl," Faith answered just as softly.

12

Now, Reva, of course I'm not telling you what you can and can't write, but I'm just letting you know that your sister called me and she's probably going to be calling your editor at Dutton if she hasn't already," Faith said in as reasonable a voice as could be expected, considering it was only 8:30 in the morning and she hadn't had her much-needed cup of coffee. She had walked twelve city blocks with Hope to the 145th Street subway station, giving her yawning sister an unheeded pep talk along the way. Hope didn't mention the truths they had shared the night before, and Faith didn't bring it up.

After making sure that Hope got on the A train heading downtown, Faith walked five blocks to Malcolm X Boulevard to catch the number 2 bus to her office. She arrived there at 7:45, thinking she'd have time to grab a cup of coffee and read *The New York Times* before the telephones started ringing off the hook. She hadn't counted on Reva Sinclair pacing back and forth in front of her office door, awaiting her arrival.

"I don't care who Wanda calls. If I want to write a book about a cum-sucking slut, than that's my business," Reva Sinclair huffed as she pulled her sable stole higher on her shoulders. She squinted, then pursed her lips at Faith, flashing her an accusing look of betrayal.

"Well, that's true, but you did name the slut Wanda—"

"So what? It's not like that's an unusual name!" Reva interrupted imperiously.

"And you do have her growing up in the Foster Projects, just like you and Wanda . . ."

"So? Those projects have been around for fifty years. There's probably a million Wandas who grew up there!" Reva raised herself to full height in the chair, so that she was actually looking down her nose at Faith as they talked.

"True, but your Wanda is in her mid-thirties, has three children by three different men, and a sister who's a best-selling novelist," Faith continued in her reasonable tone.

Reva crossed her legs, then removed a cigarette from the fourteen-carat gold case and tapped it on Faith's desk to evenly distribute the tobacco. She dropped the cigarette case back into her Gucci purse, fished out a matching cigarette lighter, lit her cigarette, and slowly exhaled a stream of smoke before looking at Faith and asking coolly, "And your point?"

"Reva!" Faith's patience was wearing thin. "You can't deny the similarities!"

"I don't know why my sister thinks my character is based on her. I mean, please, her dog is named Sheba. The Wanda in my book has a dog named Egypt." Reva rolled her eyes, her crossed leg furiously tapping air.

Faith looked across the desk at Ann for help, but her office mate pretended to be engrossed by a manuscript, although the usually emotionally reserved woman's lips were pursed, as if trying to hold back a grin. She was clearly enjoying the conversation. Faith sighed openly.

"Sweetie, all I'm saying is that it would make things so much easier if you would just give the character another name," Faith said, once again trying to reason with her rich client. "How about Barbara? That's a nice name. And maybe you can have her growing up in the Taft Projects? It would still be Harlem. And maybe . . ."

"I will not let that little slut dictate what I write!" Reva slammed a kid-gloved fist down on Faith's desk. "I'm an artist! A creative being! I have to stay true to my characters!"

"I know, honey, I know . . . and I wouldn't have it any other way. But you know, Wanda did mention that you told her, in front of witnesses, that you were going to write about her if she didn't give you some ring that belonged to your grandmother."

"That ring was supposed to go to me! Wanda stole it from my mother's jewelry box right after the funeral." Reva slammed her fist down again, rattling the telephones on the desk. "She's nothing but a no-good, thieving, low-life slut," Reva spat. "Did she also tell you that she has a hundred-dollar-a-day coke habit, and that she does lap dances for the men in her building to get money to feed that habit?"

"As does the character in your book," Faith sighed and leaned back in the chair.

"My goodness, Faith—it's a novel! She can't sue me over a novel!" Reva leaned forward in her chair and then angrily flicked her cigarette ashes into the wastepaper basket by Faith's desk.

"Reva, honey, it's been done before. Look at what happened to Terry McMillan after she wrote *Disappearing Acts*. And even if she's not successful, why tie up the book in court while the whole thing plays out? Wouldn't it be so much simpler to make just a few tiny changes?"

"I'm an artist! I can't worry myself with what this one likes or that one likes," Reva huffed. "If she doesn't like my book, she can write her own."

"All right, Reva, you know I'll support you every step of the way." Faith shrugged her shoulders and put on her best agent's smile. "But you know Dutton might get a little squeamish if she calls them . . ."

"Hah! I've made those folks a million dollars. I've had two books on the *New York Times* best-seller list, and one of my books is being made into a movie as we speak, which means more money for them." Reva stood up and adjusted her stole on her shoulders, and her mouth into a pout. "If they want to act squeamish, then fine. We'll take the book elsewhere. I know both Random House and Simon & Schuster would just love to have my next masterpiece."

Faith stood up, walked behind the desk, and clasped Reva by the shoulders.

"Well, let's see if Wanda is really going to call them, and if she does, let's see how they react before we start talking about switching publishing houses, okay?" Faith slipped her arm through Reva's as she walked to the door. "I promise I'll notify you immediately if they call me, and we'll plan a course of action from there."

"Fine. But they'd better realize what they have. I'm not just some hapless writer off the street. I'm Reva Sinclair . . ."

"And one of the best writers of our time," Faith said soothingly. "Did I say *one* of the best? I meant *the* best. You can write circles around anyone out there now."

"That's right, and you'd better remind them of that if they give us any trouble." Reva stopped and pulled out a gold compact mirror to check her makeup. Upon finding her appearance satisfactory, she dropped her compact back into her purse, tossed her head, and walked out of the office.

"Ann, would you pass me a dictionary for a moment?" Faith said as she turned back into the office. "I just want to see if Merriam Webster needs an updated picture of Reva."

"A picture of Reva?" Ann frowned.

"Um hmm, next to the word 'diva.'" The two women started laughing as Faith walked over to the coffee machine and poured a hot cup of java.

"That woman is a real character, you know. I knew when I walked in and saw her sitting at your desk that she was in the process of making your day," Ann said sympathetically.

"Yeah, she's a character all right." Faith sighed. "But she sure brings in the money."

"Isn't that the truth? Our first blockbuster book. We wouldn't have been able to pay the rent a couple of years ago if it weren't for her." Ann chuckled. "And you have to admit, it wasn't like money changed her."

"Nope, Miss Thang was a diva before she had a dime. Remember when she came in here, without an appointment, and said she was going to put our agency on the map?" Faith laughed. "She threw her manuscript on my desk and then sat down and said she'd wait while I read it."

"And, to your credit, you actually read a few chapters."

Faith smiled as she remembered. She had only intended to read a page or two to humor the woman, but found herself getting drawn into the story—a historical novel set in the Harlem Renaissance. When she finally looked up from the manuscript, twenty minutes and thirty-five pages later, she whipped out a boilerplate contract from her desk and signed Reva Sinclair on the spot. The book became part of a three-book deal with Doubleday and fetched a healthy $500,000 royalty advance.

"It was good reading." Faith stifled a yawn and then shrugged as she leafed through her telephone messages. It wasn't even 10:00 A.M. yet, and all she wanted to do was curl up in her chair and go to sleep.

"Oh, my God!"

Faith turned to look at her partner, who stood awestruck in front of her computer. She quickly walked over, spilling some of the coffee on her hand as she did so, but not noticing the pain. "What's wrong?"

"Oh my God!" Ann repeated, still in shock.

"What? What is it?" Faith looked over Ann's shoulder and read the e-mail message on the screen.

"Oh my God! We got it!" Faith started jumping up and down. *"We got it!"*

"Got what?" Faith and Ann turned as Carol bounced into the office wearing a green army jacket and a wide grin. She threw her backpack on the floor, plopped down in the chair next to Ann's desk, and swept the black beret from her head, releasing a cascade of honey-blond curls. Her face was flushed and she was slightly out of breath, as if she had walked up the three flights of stairs two steps at a time instead of taking the elevator. "What were you guys yelling about?" She turned to Ann and then Faith. "I could hear you all the way out in the hall."

"Walter Frisby! We've got Walter Frisby!" Faith danced a jig around the office. "Hoo hah!

"Walter who?"

"The writer I told you about a couple of weeks ago, who was thinking of switching agencies," Ann answered with a smile, and in a calmer tone. "But when did you get in? I thought you weren't due back for another week." She reached over and took Carol's hand in her own. "Did something happen, Carol? Is everything okay?"

Carol gave an exaggerated shrug and started giggling. "Richard got on my nerves as usual. So I left. He's such a jerk."

"I hope you didn't leave under bad terms." Ann's brow furrowed.

"Like I said, he's a jerk." Carol gave an imperious wave of her hand, and then looked back at Faith, who was furiously dialing the telephone.

"Oh, dang, Henry's not answering his cell phone." Faith held the telephone to her ear for a moment, debating whether she should leave a message, then sighed and put the telephone back on the receiver. She picked it up immediately and starting punching in her mother's telephone number, and then remembered they weren't speaking.

"Who's this writer?" Carol asked as she slumped into a swivel chair and started twirling around.

"Who is this writer, you ask? *Only Mr. Walter Frisby, the hottest African-American mystery writer on the market!*" Faith reached over and grabbed the arms of Carol's chair, temporarily stopping the spin. "*And we've got him!*" She started jumping around the office again, hooting at the top of her lungs.

Ann chuckled, then went and poured a cup of coffee, which she brought back to Carol, who gratefully took a sip.

"Wait a minute. Wait a minute." Faith rushed back to the computer screen. "Let me tell you exactly what the man said." She cleared her throat. "Dear Ms. Freeman. I hope this e-mail finds you, your family, and your partner in good health," Faith said, mimicking a man's voice. "I want you to know that I have finally come to a decision, and have chosen your agency to act as my literary representative. That's if you will still have me after all this time." Faith looked up from the screen. "Yeah, right!" she laughed.

"I've completed and turned over *Moon Hell* to my present agent, thereby completing my three-book deal with Hyperion Books. I also happen to have two completed manuscripts for which I hope you will negotiate a publishing contract. If you are interested in having me as a client, I hope you'll immediately send me a contract so I can sign it and send over these manuscripts. As you know, I can't do any negotiating with any publishers for three months per my present contract, but I think the earlier we get started talking about what kind of deal we'll be asking for, the better. I have to say that I am thoroughly pleased with my present publisher, but if they're not willing to pay a fair price, I have no reservations about shopping it around to other publishers. I think we should ask for a $2 million advance, but if you think otherwise, please let me know." Faith looked up from the computer screen again. "How much is our commission on two million? Three hundred thousand? Oh, I can definitely live with that."

"And as I'm sure you know," Faith started reading again, "my last two books were turned into movies. What do you think of us trying to simultaneously sell the book and the movie rights? Please call or e-mail me as soon as you can with your thoughts. I look forward to working with you."

Faith clutched her hands to her chest and looked up at the ceiling. "Thank you, Jesus! My prayers have been answered."

"Well, I think this calls for a celebration! Let's go have a drink!" Carol grinned.

Ann looked at her watch and frowned. "This early?"

"Why not? I bet that club on 135th Street and Adam Clayton Jr. Boulevard is open. What's the name of it again?"

"Wells Restaurant. I don't think they open until two, though," Faith said as she flipped through her Rolodex looking for Walter Frisby's telephone number. "Hey, Ann, what do you say we send a press release to *Publishers Weekly* about this? Oh man, what a coup."

"Let's wait until he actually signs the contract."

"Of course."

"And let's make sure he knows we're going to do the press release.

There may be people he'd like to inform himself, rather than having them read about it in the industry's most-read magazine."

"Of course," Faith answered again.

"Well, what about that place Henry took us to for Ann's birthday? The one down the street from here?" Carol interrupted.

"The Baby Grand? I doubt that they're open." Faith grinned when she found the telephone number. "Hey, Ann . . ."

"Carol, I was hoping you and I could go have a quiet lunch together, so you could tell me about your trip," Ann said softly, and seemingly oblivious to Faith's presence.

Uh oh, something's up, Faith thought. Why is Carol avoiding talking to Ann alone? Is there trouble in paradise? Hmm . . . aren't they supposed to be getting ready to get married? Not that anyone's told me yet.

"Oh, yeah, yeah, we're going to talk," Carol said to Ann hurriedly, with just the tiniest hint of guilt in her voice. "I just thought it would be nice if I could take you two out to celebrate the good news and all."

"Oh please, don't worry about me." Faith waved her hand in their direction. "I'm going to be doing my celebrating when Henry gets in tonight."

"Oh, but we want to. Don't we, Ann?" Carol jumped up from the chair and walked over to Faith's desk, ignoring Ann's entreaties.

"Oh! And we have two things to celebrate," Carol said excitedly. "Has Ann told you yet that she and I are getting married?"

"No, she didn't!" Faith feigned surprise. Finally! she thought. "Congratulations! When's the big day?"

"In June!" Carol said triumphantly, now that it seemed things might be going her way.

"June what? I have to put it on my calendar."

"Umm, er, June what?" Carol turned to Ann.

"June seventeenth," Ann said quietly.

"Dang, Carol, you don't even remember your own wedding date. Hey, that's my birthday!"

"Is it? Oh, I'm so sorry, but that's the only weekend that was available in June." Ann's hands flew to her mouth and her distress was evident. "And we really wanted to have a June wedding."

"Oh, well, that's fine." Faith grinned. "I couldn't imagine a better way to spend my birthday than watching my partner get hitched."

"Ooh, and I want you to be my maid of honor!" Carol said excitedly. "We can go shopping for dresses together. You know I love your taste in clothes!"

"Oh, Carol. That's such an honor! I'd love to!" Faith smiled as she spoke, but she couldn't hide her astonishment. Ann asking her to be in the wedding wouldn't have been surprising, but while she and Carol were friendly, they weren't all that close.

"Good, then it's settled! So where are we going to celebrate?" Carol asked excitedly.

"Well, I'm not going anywhere until I call Walter Frisby and find out where he wants me to send the contract." Faith reached for the phone and began tapping the keypad with her pen. "And besides, someone should probably stay in the office. Why don't you guys go ahead and just bring me back a doggie bag."

Ann picked up Carol's army jacket and handed it to her, then went to the coat rack and put on a beige cashmere coat. "That sounds like a great idea, Faith." She looked at Carol pointedly. "Are you ready?"

"Um, yeah." Carol slowly put on her jacket, then adjusted the beret on her head and walked to the door with Ann.

"Hey," she turned back to Faith suddenly. "What about tonight? Maybe the four of us could go out and celebrate tonight? You and Henry, and Ann and me?"

"No, I'm going to pass. Henry's flying home tonight and I want to keep him all to myself, if you know what I mean," Faith said with a smile.

"I certainly do know what you mean," Ann said pointedly. "Carol, are you ready *now*?"

Hmmm . . . something deep is going on there, Faith thought as Carol reluctantly followed Ann out of the office. Faith waited impatiently for her prospective client to pick up the telephone. Damn, the answering machine.

"Hi Walter, this is Faith Freeman. I just got your e-mail and I can't tell you how thrilled I am that you've decided to sign with me. Please call and give me your address and I'll have a messenger drop off a contract for you to sign this afternoon. You'll see it's a pretty standard contract, but please let me know if there's any language that troubles you, and I'm sure we can work it out. Thanks for everything, and I look forward to working with you."

Faith looked up at the clock after she put the telephone down. It was only 9:30. She started sifting through the stack of query letters in her in-basket, glancing down at the pile of manuscripts on the floor. May as well get some work done. She sighed as she sat down, deciding to read a few of the unsolicited manuscripts before getting to the query letters.

When she opened her business, Faith had hired Hope to help her read manuscripts, since her twin had also been a voracious reader. But that was before her sister had become totally wrapped up in the street life. When they were in elementary school, Hope had said she wanted to be a nurse. By the time Hope was thirteen, she confided to Faith that she aspired to be a call girl. Faith thought it was a bad joke at the time. How can someone go from wanting to be a nurse to a call girl? It just didn't make sense. Now, look at the way things have turned out. Hope smoking crack and turning street tricks for five or ten dollars, and hoping none of her johns strangle or stab her in the process. Faith shuddered. At least if she were a call girl, she'd have a better class of clientele. She sighed and tried to concentrate on the manuscript in front of her. She set it aside after reading just the first few pages. Bad grammar, filled with typos, and a boring plot.

It was almost 1:00 before Faith took a break. None of the seven manuscripts she had skimmed through were promising, so those she unceremoniously dumped in the trash after removing the self-addressed, stamped envelope from the packaging so she could send a form rejection letter to the author. She always personalized the rejection letters for manuscripts that she requested, but unsolicited manuscripts only warranted form letters, and that's only if they were smart enough to enclose the self-addressed, stamped envelope. She knew some agents who didn't even bother with form letters for unsolicited manuscripts, and she didn't blame them. If the authors had sent query letters before sending their manuscripts, which was the accepted practice, they could have saved themselves a lot of unnecessary postage, and saved the agents a lot of time.

Of the seventy-five query letters Faith went through that morning, five seemed promising. She set four of them aside, planning on calling the authors later in the day to ask them to send a synopsis and the first three chapters of their manuscripts. The fifth query letter was going to present a problem because the author had somehow neglected to include a return address or telephone number. She looked at the postmark on the envelope: Eufala, Alabama. She decided to call long distance information. After all, there couldn't possibly be that many Theotis Bowens in a small town like that, and he did send a really intriguing query letter. Brilliant enough to write a catchy query letter, absentminded enough not to have sent a return address.

"Hey, Baby Girl! Get ready to cruise the seven seas!"

Hope strode through the door, plopped down in a swivel chair, and twirled the seat around to prop her feet up on Faith's desk, almost all in one motion. Faith pushed her sister's feet back down to the floor.

"So, you got the job, huh? Congrats."

"Like there was really any doubt," Hope snorted. "I start bright and early Monday morning. And there ain't no dress code, so I can wear jeans and sneakers if I want."

Faith shook her head in exasperation. "No dress code doesn't mean jeans and sneakers, Hope. But . . . whatever. Just, please, keep this job, okay?"

"Okay. Where's Ann?"

"She and Carol went out to lunch. I would have thought they'd be back by now. That's something about them getting married, huh?"

"Yeah, Ann called me and told me last week when I was at Mommy's. Dang, I forgot to tell Mommy." Hope shrugged. "Oh, well."

"Hmph, Mommy knows already. Seems like everyone knew but me. Well, guess what? I'm going to be the maid of honor!"

"Old news."

"You already knew?"

"Yep. I'm going to be one of Carol's bridesmaids. Ann asked me when she told me about the wedding. You eat yet? I'm hungry."

Faith stood up from her desk and reached for her coat. "Now that doesn't really make any sense. Why would Carol want you for a bridesmaid?"

"Hey! What you trying to say?" Hope said indignantly.

"No offense, but you guys aren't even friends, really. I mean, I thought it was a stretch when she asked me to be the maid of honor, but I think that's at least more understandable than asking you to be a bridesmaid. It's not like she doesn't have her own circle of friends.

You'd think she'd ask some of those ditzy PETA folks she hangs out with."

"Huh, she knows better than to invite them to the same wedding where you're going to be. What do you think they'd do if they threw a can of paint on this bad leather coat you wearing, or that new fur coat you love so much?"

"I'd kick their ass," Faith said dryly as they waited for the elevator. "I'd chase them down and kick their ass, and then stick their head in a can of paint and drown the bitches. Then I'd hang them, naked, from the nearest lamppost and use their tiny limp dicks for target practice. Then I'd—" Faith stopped suddenly, realizing she was getting carried away. "Anyway, it doesn't matter, because I won't be wearing a fur coat. The wedding is in June."

"Yeah, on our birthday. At least I won't forget."

"And, oh! Listen, can you make yourself scarce tonight? Henry's coming home and I wanted to have a private celebration."

Hope pursed her lips. "Yeah," she said slowly, "I guess I can find a spot for the night. What's up, though? What you guys celebrating?"

"Well, we just got word that Walter Frisby has picked us as his new agents, but . . ." Faith lowered her eyes with a smile, "the truth is, I just want to spend some quality time with him. He's been so supportive of everything's that's been going on between you, me, and Mommy, and I just want to remind him how much I appreciate him."

"Spare me the mushy stuff," Hope snorted. "Yeah, I'll ask Susan if I can stay over her house. I bet she can use the company. She still hasn't let Jason back in the house, you know. Cheating bastard."

Faith nodded her head in admiration of Susan, as well as Hope. Many women would have second thoughts about telling their girlfriend they had seen their man with another woman—there's always a chance that your girlfriend won't believe you and then turn on you. Or worse, they could believe you and still turn on you. But Hope disregarded Faith's caution and called Susan that evening. Ironically, Susan knew about what had happened at the restaurant before she spoke to Hope. Another friend of hers had been there and called to tell her that Jason was smooching with some skinny chick, and also about the scene that Hope had made on Susan's behalf. And Jason was so sure that Hope was going to tell that he confessed as soon as he got home that evening. The girl was his secretary, Jason said, and Hope had gotten it all wrong and made an unwarranted ado. Susan listened quietly while Jason related his side of the story, and remained silent while Jason urged her to drop Hope as a friend, since "that woman" had problems. It wasn't until he finished his tale and went to take Susan into his arms that she went off on him, ultimately breaking two of his ribs with the heavy skillet that was on the kitchen counter. Later, Susan told Hope that he should have been glad that she hadn't actually started cooking yet, because otherwise that pan would have been filled with hot grease. When Hope called that evening, Susan thanked her over and over for "having her back" in her time of need. She had suspected Jason was too close to his secretary, but had had no proof until that day.

"I've got to hand it to Susan, as crazy as she was about Jason, she put a quick end to that crap," Faith said. "I don't know what I would have done in the same situation."

"Puleeze! Like Henry has eyes for anyone but you. He's the most lovesick puppy I've ever met," Hope snorted. "Even after all these years, he still acts like he's in the middle of a high school crush."

Faith grinned. "Yeah. That's cool, because I sure do have a crush on my baby."

"Didn't I just ask you to spare me the mushies?" Hope rolled her eyes. "But anyway, like I was saying, I'll just go on over and stay with Susan. I know she's real lonely and stuff." Hope nodded. "She'll probably appreciate the company. But how 'bout we celebrate my new job tomorrow night, since you gonna be doing the cootchy-coo with Henry tonight?"

"Naw, Baby Girl." Faith shook her head. "I promised myself I'd go over to Mommy's and make up with her. I just hope she'll talk to me. It's been almost a week now without us talking. I'm hoping she's calmed down."

"She has. I just came from there."

"You did?" Faith was astonished. "And she let you in?"

"Yeah, I guess what we've been talking about the last week or so's been getting to me, so I just went over there to kinda make my peace and stuff." Hope shifted uncomfortably in her chair. "But she won't even mention what happened when we was all over there, and kept trying to change the subject when I tried to talk about it. But she's all sorry and stuff, you can tell. She even said I should move back in if I want to."

"Get out of here!"

"Yeah. I guess we all making some kinda breakthrough or something, huh?"

"I guess." Faith shook her head. "Well, congratulations on taking the first step with Mommy."

"Hey, there's something else you gotta congratulate me for," Hope interrupted her sister's thoughts.

"What's that?"

"I joined an outpatient drug program. You know, that one on 128th and Park Avenue."

"Get out of here!" Faith's mouth dropped open in surprise. She was hoping that their talk the night before might motivate Hope to get her act together, but she didn't think she'd really get the message this quickly.

"Yeah, I figured if I'm gonna be trying to straighten myself out, I might as well really try to straighten myself out," Hope said, as if reading Faith's mind. "Umm, and I wanted to tell you that I'm glad we actually talked last night. It made me see things in a different way and stuff."

"It was a very important talk and I'm glad we had it, too," Faith responded cautiously. The night before was obviously a major break-through and she was afraid to push too far, but . . . "but I want you to think about getting some counseling, too, Hope. It's one thing for us to talk about it, but I do think you need to talk to a professional."

"Aw Faith, come on! I just got a job, went and made my peace with Mommy, and joined a drug program all in one day." Hope rolled her eyes and slouched down in the chair. "And I don't see why I gotta be talking to no counselor anyway. I got you if I need to talk and stuff."

"You sure do, Baby Girl, but it might help to share things with someone besides me, okay?" Faith said soothingly. "I'm not saying to-day or anything, but it's something you should consider for the fu-ture."

"Yeah, whatever . . ." Hope grumbled. "Come on . . . at least I'm gonna get you to treat me to lunch."

13

Faith studied the wine list as she waited for Henry to arrive at Patsy's Restaurant. She had wanted a quiet night at home, but Henry had called from the airport, and when she told him about landing the Frisby account, he insisted they go out to celebrate. He suggested Patsy's, since they hadn't had Italian food in a while and Patsy's was the best Italian restaurant in Harlem—although technically it was in East Harlem. It was an old hangout of Frank Sinatra's, and rumor had it that the famous New York mob boss Lucky Luciano had entertained Al Capone there back in the 1920s.

Patsy's was classic Italian—the red and white gingham tablecloth with the white candle melting down into an empty green wine bottle. Henry had taken care of the reservations, and when Faith arrived at 7:30 sharp as he had insisted, she was immediately escorted to a small table near the back of the restaurant. Her companion, the heavily accented maitre d' said, had called to say he would be late. "But please to have some wine while you wait, signorina. Antonio, wassa da matta wit you? Bringa the lovely signorina some bread."

Wonderful service. We've got to eat here more often. Faith decided on a bottle of Beringer White Zinfandel knowing that Henry would probably order his usual fare, calamari. She was kind of in the mood for seafood herself.

"Excuse me, Miss. Is this seat taken?"

Faith looked up in surprise to see a tall, light-complexioned man bending over the table and flashing a huge smile. He was wearing a dark brown leather coat over an expensive-looking dark brown business suit, with a cream-colored shirt and a brown print tie. Faith scanned her mental file, trying to put a name to the face, but she drew a blank.

"I don't mean to bother you," the man placed his hand over Faith's and she could see the glint of a gold Rolex watch, "but I just hate to see a woman as lovely as you dining alone."

Faith slipped her hand away. "I'm sorry, but I don't know you, and I . . ."

"Mr. Olsen, please, not to bother the signorina!" The maitre d' was at the man's side, trying to pull him away. "Please, signor, let me show you to a very nice table near a window. Please."

The man looked at the maitre d' with amusement. "Calm down, Nuncio. I was just going to introduce myself to the young lady." He turned back to Faith. "Miss, I didn't mean to disturb you, but as I was saying . . ."

"No, no, no, Signor Olsen," the maitre d' was pulling the man's arm frantically. "You don't understand. You must not disturb this signorina. Come. I introduce you to very nice young lady."

You must not disturb this signorina? What the hell is going on here? she thought. Faith's mouth hung open as she looked from the maitre d' to the impetuous stranger. She slid her chair from the table.

"No, no, signorina, please do not get up." The maitre d' seemed near tears. "I promise you, you will not be disturbed. Antonio, Antonio, bring the signorina a bottle of our finest wine." He turned to the man again. "Signor Olsen. I must insist that you come away now before it is too late."

Too late? What the hell . . .

Suddenly she saw a tall man in a black suit and tie with a long black cashmere coat thrown over his shoulders and a black fedora pulled down low over his face approaching the table, flanked by two burly men, who could only be described as goons.

"Is there a problem here, Nuncio?" the fedoraed man asked in a low but familiar voice. Faith blinked wildly. Henry?

"Don Enrique!" The maitre d' turned to the man—to Henry. "No, no problem, signor," he sputtered. "This signor was just paying his respects to the signorina. He is now finished and we go away." He started pulling at the man again. "Come, Signor Olsen. We go away."

The man pulled his arm away indignantly. "Sorry if there's some misunderstanding, I just wanted to introduce myself. I'm Jeremy Olsen." He extended his arm out to Henry as if to shake hands. But one of the burly men stepped in front of him.

"Now look, I don't want any trouble . . ."

The burly man glanced at Henry as if awaiting a signal. The arch of Henry's eyebrow sufficed, and to Faith's astonishment, the burly man grabbed the stranger by the scruff of the neck and started hauling the man toward the exit.

"Hey, let go of me. Someone call the police!" The man yelled, as he was heaved through the door.

"Don Enrique, please. A thousand apologies. I do not believe someone let that piece of dirt into my establishment," the maitre d' sputtered as he rushed to remove the coat from Henry's shoulders. "I will fire the man who let him in. A hundred curses on him and his whore of a mother for bearing him."

Henry coolly raised his hand, signaling the sniveling man to stop. "Nuncio, it is of no consequence."

"Of course, Don Enrique, of no consequence at all," the maitre d' answered quickly.

"Don Enrique? What the . . ." Faith's mind was racing.

Henry took off his hat, and the second burly man took the hat and pulled out a chair for Henry to sit in. Faith gasped. Henry's dark brown Afro was gone, replaced by a slick, jet black perm, a la Billy Dee Williams. And his mustache, which had always been on the thin side, was cut into a skinny line reminiscent of Marlon Brando in *The Godfather*. Faith held her napkin to her mouth, trying to suppress her giggles. This man knows how to put on an act, she thought.

Henry pulled out a Cuban cigar from the breast pocket of his shirt, and the burly man and the maitre d' both flashed cigarette lighters in front of him. It was too much for Faith, who had been sitting through the scene in quiet astonishment. She started to giggle uncontrollably and then broke into a full laughter. Soon, tears were rolling down her cheeks and she had to stop herself from sliding down her chair and onto the floor.

"Will you be having your usual, Don Enrique?" the maitre d' had to almost shout to be heard over Faith's laughter.

"Yes, Nuncio. Now, that will be all." He extended his hand and the maitre d' bent down to solemnly kiss it.

"Very good, Godfather," he said reverently.

"Godfather!" Faith hooted. "Oh, God, I can't take it!" She started pounding the table in a vain attempt to regain her composure. "Stop it. You're killing me."

"Faith, my beloved. You're making a scene," Henry said calmly as he exhaled the aromatic cigar smoke.

"Oh? I'm the one making a scene!" Faith was laughing so hard she could barely speak. "Oh, Henry. You are too much. I can't believe you went through all this."

Henry brought Faith's hand to his lips and kissed it softly. Then he looked her deeply in the eyes, before finally breaking into a big grin. "Admit it, baby. Robert De Niro and Al Pacino ain't got shit on me."

14

So that's why Henry was looking like Shaquille O'Neal when I saw him this morning, huh? He shaved his head to get the perm out?" Hope was laughing hysterically as Faith related the events of the night before. "Damn, I wish I had seen him!"

"Hey, the man looked good! Kinda like Billy Dee in *Lady Sings the Blues*." Faith couldn't help but laugh along with her sister. Forget the fact that the other people in the restaurant were looking at them like they had both lost their minds.

"Man, you should write a book about some of the stuff you and Henry be pulling." Hope shook her head. "Both of ya'll are crazy as all shit."

Faith shrugged her shoulders and grinned. "It works for us."

"Yeah, it sure seems to and stuff." Hope continued to chuckle as she picked up her menu.

"So, I know you got something planned for him when he gets back from Chicago. He's leaving tomorrow, right?"

"Yeah," Faith sighed. Henry's firm had decided to invest in the publishing house in Chicago, and Henry had to go out and finalize the arrangements. And since he was going to be out in the Midwest anyway, his firm wanted him to meet with a hosiery company in Detroit. The whole trip would take about a week, the longest they'd ever been away from each other. At least Hope was going to be there to keep her company.

"I'm telling you, Faith, you so busy selling other people's books to publishers and you have a best-seller on your hands. *How to Keep the Magic Alive*."

"Yeah, and I know at least two people who should read it," Faith grunted. "I swear, I don't see this wedding coming off in June. I have a feeling Carol is getting ready to move on."

"Naw, you've gots to have that wrong. Ain't you supposed to be going with Carol to pick out a wedding dress tomorrow?"

"No, we already picked out the wedding dress." Faith took a sip of water. "We're looking at bridesmaid dresses."

"Well, make sure they're nice. I don't want us to be looking like clowns on our own birthday."

"I'm telling you, Hope, there isn't going to be a wedding." Faith signaled for the waiter.

"So why don't you think there's going to be a wedding?" Hope demanded once they had ordered.

"Because Ann has been acting gloomy all week and twice I've heard her on the telephone acting like she's almost pleading with Carol to stay." Faith sighed through her teeth. It had pained her tremendously to hear Ann so distressed. In her view, if anyone should be begging, it should be Carol. But then it was always Ann that did the work in that relationship, as far as Faith could see. It was Ann that had been footing the bills in that house, and Ann that made all the vacation arrangements, and Ann that did just about everything. All Carol did was volunteer for crazy social projects, pledging a little bit of her time and a lot of Ann's money until she became distracted and moved on to the next crazy project.

"Get outta here! That's a damn shame." Hope shook her head. "And here all this time I thought they was so in love."

"I don't know. I've always gotten the impression that it's Ann that's in love and Carol that loves having Ann in love with her." Faith sighed. "Ann is so sensible when it comes to everyone and everything except her own relationship."

"Maybe you should talk to her." Hope suggested.

"No. I know Ann, and I know that she would be mortified if she thought I knew that she was having trouble at home." Faith shook her head. "But don't think the thought didn't cross my mind. Sometimes I feel like slapping some sense into that stupid Carol."

Hope snorted. "Look at you, the maid of honor calling the bride stupid."

"Yeah, well. We'll see." Faith sucked her teeth. "I can't be a maid of honor if they call off the wedding. Oh, but, Hope, you should see the wedding dress! It's stunning!"

"Get outta here." Hope laughed. "I woulda thought Carol woulda wanted to go get married in army boots. That's my girl, but she's crazy as shit."

Faith shrugged. "You're not going to believe this, but Carol didn't really seem to care what she wore. In fact, I wound up picking the dress out for her. I'm telling you, that girl isn't planning on getting married."

"Oh yeah," Hope said a little later as she was eating her chili con carne, "didn't you say you were going to ask Ann why they were keeping the wedding a secret from you in the beginning?"

"Well, yeah, but I haven't, because I didn't want to stress her out any more than she is already," Faith said as she ate the potato chips that came with her cheeseburger. "But I figure it's because she wanted to take me out to dinner and make a big production out of the announcement, and she just hadn't gotten around to it."

"Anyway," Hope shrugged her shoulders, "not to change the subject, but I just want you to know that I love the job so far. I think I'm going to keep this one."

"Oh, that's good," Faith snorted. "Now let's see, how long have you been there? One day? Oh, nope. Half a day. I'll be pleased if you manage to go back after lunch and finish the day."

"Very funny!" Hope grinned. "Seriously, though, I can tell I'm gonna like it there. And my boss says she loves my attitude."

"Your bosses always love your attitude, Hope. That's why they always trip when you suddenly quit without giving them a reason."

"Oh my God! Faith!" Hope gasped and leaned so far over the table her chest touched tomato sauce from the chili as she tried to whisper to her sister. "You're just not going to believe who's sitting up in here with another woman!"

"What? Jason again?" Faith scanned the restaurant, trying to spot him.

"Stop looking, they'll see you!" Hope said urgently. "It's not Jason!"

"Who then?" Faith turned to Hope, still trying to glance around the restaurant with her peripheral vision.

"It's Carol!" Hope said in a loud whisper. "And we were just talking about her, too."

Faith swung around in her chair, ignoring Hope's protestations, and saw that it was indeed Carol, sitting across the room at a corner booth and laughing with a good-looking middle-aged redhead. Carol's army jacket and black beret were thrown carelessly over the chair next to her, but the woman's expensive-looking green wool coat was neatly hung on the steel coat hook attached to the side of the booth. Faith couldn't help but note that it was the same kind of coat Ann would wear.

"Okay, no shit," Hope interrupted Faith's thoughts with her loud whisper. "Tell me if that's not a red-headed version of Ann. She's even wearing a scarf around her neck like Ann."

The waitress appeared before Faith could answer. "Would you like anything else?"

"Naw, you can bring us the bill. I gotta get back to work anyway," Hope said. "You gonna say anything to her?" she asked Faith after the waitress was paid and they gathered up their coats.

Faith nodded as she headed in the direction of Carol and her red-headed friend. "But stay cool," she said to Hope over her shoulder. "Let's find out what's really going on here before you decide to make a scene. They just might be friends or something."

"Please." Hope rolled her eyes. "Me? Make a scene?"

"Hey! I didn't know you guys eat here!" Carol jumped up from the table and hugged Faith and then Hope. "I want to introduce you to my mother. Sandra, this is Faith, and this is Hope," she said turning to the middle-aged woman. Faith tried to keep a straight face as she shook the woman's hand. Her resemblance to Ann was uncanny. Even the slight widow's peak, the pale skin, and the large, blue eyes. I've heard of men who hook up with women because they look like their mother, but lesbians do that, too? Then again, why not? Seems kind of freaky, though.

"Oh, dang, and here we thought you was having an affair or something." Hope laughed. "How you doing, Sandra? Dang, I wish my mother would let me call her by her first name."

"Nice to meet you both," Sandra said icily, a tone that Faith could see failed to register with Hope.

"You know, you look just like someone I know," Hope said, rubbing her chin as if trying to figure out who.

"It was nice meeting you, too." Faith grabbed Hope's arm and tried to pull her toward the door.

"That's it." Hope snapped her fingers. "She looks just like Ann, doesn't she, Faith?" She turned back to Sandra. "I guess you know Ann . . . your daughter's fiancé?" She gave Faith her most innocent look and asked, "Would that be fiancé with one 'e' for male or two 'e's for female?"

"Ooh, Hope." Carol was laughing at her mother's discomfort. "You just crack me up! Doesn't she just crack you up, Sandra?"

"She's simply hilarious," Sandra said in a tone even frostier than before.

"And you know something even funnier?" Hope leaned in close to Sandra. "When I first saw the two of you, I thought Carol was cheating on Ann. Isn't that something?"

"Hope, come on," Faith said sharply.

"Ooh, Hope, you are just too much." Carol was really laughing now. "You thought Sandra was my lover. Ooh, that's just too much."

"We're sorry for disturbing your lunch, Sandra." Faith cut her eyes at both Carol and Hope. "How long will you be in town?"

"Just for the week." Sandra started slicing into the large steak in front of her, likely hoping—Faith thought—that she would rather be slicing Hope's neck.

"Well, how would we know she's your mother? You coulda been creeping on our girl, Ann." Hope giggled as she tapped Carol on the arm.

"Oh honey, please." Carol put her hands on her skinny hips and tried to shake her little butt. "If I was cheating on Ann, I'd be with a man!"

Faith blinked. What? She started to say something to Carol, but Hope was too quick.

"Oh no you didn't, girlfriend," Hope said in her most ghettofied voice, obviously trying to egg Carol on. "Don't tell me you're a switch-hitter."

"Honey, please. I'm going to tell you now, I like me a little meat every now and then." Carol slapped Hope on the back. "You know what I mean, girlfriend."

"Ooh, yeah, girl, tell me about it." Hope grinned.

"Anyway, it was nice meeting you, Sandra," Faith said politely as she tugged on Hope's arm again. "I'm sorry we have to leave so soon, but my sister's got to get back to work."

"The pleasure was mine," Sandra said without looking up from her plate.

15

Could this day get any worse? Faith wondered as she buzzed the bell to her apartment. First she left her keys in the cab she took to work, which meant she couldn't get in the office, and today, of all days, Ann decided to come in late. Then, Walter Frisby called and wanted to go over every item in his contract, one by one, which took almost two hours. Then, Reva Sinclair popped in unexpectedly, complaining about her sister, her new book cover, and the state of international affairs. It took Faith another hour to get her calmed down and out of the office. And she had promised Henry she'd be home in time to ride with him to the airport. She looked at her watch: 1:00 P.M. She was running more than half an hour late. And wouldn't you know it, the telephone cable was down and none of the phones in her apartment building were working, so she couldn't get in touch with Henry to tell him she was running late. And she couldn't reach him on his cell phone, because it was turned off, which meant he probably didn't know the phones in the apartment weren't working. It was strange that Henry hadn't tried to call her, though. She buzzed the bell again. And damn if Mr. Carpenter wasn't at his usual post at the lobby desk. The old man must have decided to take a long lunch.

"Lost your keys? Let me get that for you."

Faith breathed a sigh of relief as one of her neighbors unlocked the lobby door. She quickly thanked him, then darted upstairs rather than wait on the elevator. Maybe Henry's still home waiting, she prayed. Maybe he's in the bathroom and couldn't get to the buzzer.

She pounded on the apartment door for almost two minutes before finally giving up. Damn, she thought, we didn't even get a chance to say good-bye.

"Hey, Faith?"

Faith swung around to find Hope holding the apartment door ajar.

"What are you doing here?"

"I came home to meet Henry." Faith stepped inside the apartment. "Is he still here?"

"No. He left about fifteen minutes ago," Hope said in a subdued voice.

"So what are you doing here? And in your nightgown?" Faith asked as she sunk onto the living room sofa, her coat still on. Dang, all this rushing and she had still missed him. "Why aren't you at work?"

"I overslept because you didn't wake me up." Hope sat on the love seat, opposite her sister, her eyes averted.

"I had to leave early to get some things done in the office. I set the alarm clock for you." Faith shook her head. Hope hadn't been at the job three days and already she was messing up.

"I didn't hear it," Hope said softly.

"Well, Henry must have heard it, as light as he sleeps. He didn't wake you up?" Why was Hope acting like she had just lost her best friend? It never bothered her before when she blew a gig. And why was her hair all disheveled as if she had just been in a fight?

"He tried." Hope shrugged her shoulders.

"And?"

"You know how hard it is to wake me up sometimes." Hope shrugged again. Faith looked at her suspiciously. It wasn't like Henry to give up so easily, especially since he wanted Hope to keep this job more than anyone, so she could move out of their apartment. And why did the apartment, Faith suddenly noticed, smell like someone had just sprayed a whole can of air freshener in the air?

"So, how long have you been up?" Faith got up and walked into the bedroom as she spoke. Everything seemed in place. The bed was freshly made, but Henry always did that when he was the last one to leave.

"About an hour ago," Hope answered.

"So why are you still in your nightgown?" Faith walked into the guest room. The air freshener scent was even heavier in there. The bed looked as if someone, or some ones, had been wrestling in it. Wrestling or something else? Faith tried to push the thought out of her mind, as she walked back into the living room. What was Hope doing that kept her so busy that she couldn't ring the outside buzzer when I rang the bell? Was she trying to clean up after herself?

"Why are you still in your nightgown?" Faith asked again.

"I was just getting ready to step into the shower." Hope's voice was directed at the floor.

"Uh huh, is that right?" Faith took off her coat and hung it up in the hallway closet as she tried to collect her thoughts. Hope got up from the love seat and headed toward the bathroom. "Sit back down," Faith said quietly. Hope sniffled, then went back to the love seat.

"So," Faith sat down on the couch and looked directly at her sister, who avoided her eyes, "is there anything you want to talk to me about?"

"Well," Hope started wringing her hands, "I guess I'd like to say I'm sorry."

Faith tried to keep her breathing under control as her heart beat wildly in her chest. "Sorry for what, sis?"

"I'm sorry for what happened between me and Henry." Hope started crying softly, burying her face in her hands.

"I see," Faith said in a calm voice that belied her raging emotions. "And what exactly happened between you and Henry that you feel so sorry about?"

"It wasn't my fault," Hope sobbed. "He started it. He came in the room to wake me up, and then he started kissing me and stuff. And the next thing I knew we were doing it."

It felt like someone was pressing down on her shoulders and her chest. The weight was so heavy, Faith had to struggle to take quick, shallow breaths, as if she were in the midst of labor. But she had to remain calm. She had to find out what happened. Find out how it could have happened. Find out how it could have happened to her. Henry would never hurt her like this. But he had, the evidence was staring her right in the face. How long had it been going on? Had they been messing around with each other before Hope moved in? Had the two of them been sneaking around behind her back for years?

"It was the first time it happened," Hope said between sobs as if reading her twin's mind. "And both of us were sorry as soon as we were done. Henry made me promise not to tell, and I wouldn't have if you hadn't popped in like this."

Faith leaned back and closed her eyes. That's it. This is a dream. I'm going to open my eyes in a minute and Henry's going to be right next to me, and I'm going to find out that I haven't even woken up yet this morning. This whole thing, this whole day, is just a dream.

Her eyes flew open as she felt Hope trying to grab her into a hug.

"Faith, I'm so sorry. I don't know how this could have happened!" Hope cried hysterically.

The weight suddenly lifted, Faith pushed her sister away with one hand, and the other one, balled into a fist, slammed into Hope's mouth. *"You don't know how it happened!"* she yelled as Hope fell screaming to the floor. *"You don't know how it happened?"* She slammed her fist into Hope's left eye, the full weight of her body behind the punch. She grabbed Hope from the floor and slammed her into the entertainment center. The CD player and porcelain knick-knacks crashed to the floor as she slammed Hope into it over and over again. *"You don't know how it happened?"* she continued to scream.

"Faith, stop. Please, I'm sorry!" Hope's nightgown ripped in Faith's hands as she scrambled to get away.

"You're sorry?" Faith ran after Hope, grabbing her by the hair just as she tried to shut the bathroom door. *"You're sorry?"*

Hope desperately clawed at Faith's face, as the enraged woman tried to choke her. "Faith, stop! Please! Let me go!"

"Let you go?" Faith started banging her head on the edge of commode. *"Let you go?"*

"Oh, my God!" she heard Henry's voice cry out behind her. "Faith, you're going to kill her!"

"That's right. And as soon as I'm finished I'm going to kill you!" Blood spurted from Hope's mouth and head onto Faith's hands. She tried unsuccessfully to maintain her grip on Hope's throat as Henry picked her up in the air. She twisted her body to face him, then let out a howl and tried to claw his eyes out. Henry dropped her and backed away. "What the hell is wrong with you?" he yelled.

"You fuck my sister in my house and you ask me what's wrong with

me?" She tried to smash her fist into his face, but he ducked and somehow managed to get behind her, pinning her arms behind her back.

"*Let go of me, you fucking bastard. You fucking bastard,*" she howled. "*You two-timing no good bastard!*"

"I'm not going to let you go until you calm down!" Henry half-dragged, half-carried her into the living room. "And I didn't fuck your sister! What kind of man do you think I am?"

"You liar! You fucking liar!" Faith's voice was hoarse with tears. "She confessed. She told me what you did. You no-good bastard! Let go of me."

"Well, then she's lying." Henry threw Faith down on the couch. "Hope, get your ass in here," he yelled.

"If she's lying why did someone spray air freshener all over the house to get out the smell of sex?" Faith jumped back up and tried to claw at Henry's face. "Why are the sheets all messed up? And why aren't you in Chicago, anyway? At your precious meeting! You're probably screwing some girl there, too."

"Faith, stop it. My flight was canceled, and I'm not screwing around with anyone." Henry caught her hands in his and forced her back onto the couch. "You've got to calm down."

"How can you tell me to calm down when you've been fucking my sister? How could you do this to me, Henry?" Faith started sobbing. "I trusted you."

"You can still trust me, baby." Henry pulled Faith into his arms. "You've got to believe me. I didn't do anything. I swear. Hope came on to me, but I turned her down, and that's the honest to God truth."

"Then why would Hope say you did it?" Faith demanded through her tears. "Why did she confess?"

"I don't know, Faith," Henry said soothingly. "Your sister's sick, baby. Why does she do any of the things she does?"

"Oh, I'm sick, huh?" Faith and Henry looked up to see Hope standing over them, bloody and wild-eyed, and shaking with anger. "I'm so sick I guess I just imagined this, too?" She threw something that landed on Henry's face. Faith gasped when she realized what it was: a sopping-wet used condom.

"Oh shit!" Henry wiped his face, and his mouth twisted with rage when he realized what she had thrown. "You little bitch!" He leapt up from the couch and tried to slap Hope, but the woman was too quick for him. She darted back into the bathroom and locked the door behind her.

"Get out here, you little slut!" Henry pounded the door. "You little bitch. Get out here!"

Henry didn't even notice Faith put on her coat and open the apartment door to leave.

"Miss Freeman, are you okay? I've been knocking on your door for at least five minutes. We could hear the screaming all the way down here in the lobby!" The look on Mr. Carpenter's face reminded Faith of how she must look, but she didn't care. "I done called the cops, I did," he continued, "I thought someone was getting killed."

"Mr. Carpenter, please, could you get me a cab?" she said with as much dignity as she could muster. "I just really need to leave."

16

Sweetie, if I could take the pain from your heart by taking it in my own, I would. I can't bear to see you like this. You've got to get yourself together."

Faith was slouched down in the dirty armchair, staring vacantly at the television set, barely noticing her mother as she snapped the television tray in place in front of her.

"Look, Faith, I made you some nice chicken soup. Homemade, just the way you like it." Miss Irene placed the bowl of steaming soup on the tray. "Come on, sweetie, eat a little for me."

Faith shook her head, not bothering to speak. There didn't seem much worth speaking about lately. There didn't seem to be much worth hearing. There just didn't seem to be much worth living for. It had been a week since she left the apartment on Edgecomb Avenue and she hadn't been back. She spent the first five days at a downtown hotel, where she stared at the ceiling. She didn't call anyone to let them know where she was. She'd even thrown her cell phone out of the window because it wouldn't stop ringing. She'd finally called her mother on the sixth day because she knew she was probably worried sick about her, and her mother begged and cried over the telephone for Faith to come over. She cried more when she saw Faith's condition. She hadn't showered since she left and her clothes were still spotted with dried blood, her hair matted to her head.

Miss Irene had run a warm bath for Faith and valiantly tried to fight the tears as she helped Faith take off her clothes and ease into the tub. She even washed Faith, as if she were three years old again, then dried her off. Faith didn't protest. She didn't have the strength to protest or fight anyone. She was running on automatic pilot, but just barely.

"I called Ann and told her you were over here," Miss Irene was saying as she adjusted the pillow behind Faith's head. "She was so worried about you. I told her you were okay and just needed some time away from the office. Don't you worry about a thing, she has everything under control. Oh, and she said to tell you that Walter Frisby finally signed that contract."

Why would Ann be worried? Faith wondered idly. Has someone told her what happened? Oh, I'm acting crazy. Ann's probably just worried because I haven't been in the office all week, that's all. Not that it mattered if Ann knew. It didn't matter who knew. Nothing mattered anymore.

"I'm so sorry Hope hurt you like this." Miss Irene rubbed Faith's cold hands, trying to bring life back into her daughter. "I'm glad you put her in the hospital. You just should have put her there for a month instead of three days." If Miss Irene hadn't gotten a call from the hospital, she would never have known what had happened. And she still didn't know everything. When she rushed to the hospital and Hope wouldn't say who had beat her up, and then Henry started calling every fifteen minutes looking for Faith, Miss Irene started putting two and two together.

Miss Irene brought a spoonful of soup to Faith's mouth. "Come on, sweetie, at least take a couple of spoonfuls. Please? Do it for me?"

Faith just closed her eyes and shook her head. Miss Irene sighed.

"Henry's been calling here every fifteen minutes. He's crazy with worry, Faith."

Faith looked up at her mother and her eyes brimmed with tears. "I don't want to see him, Mommy."

"I know, sweetie. You don't have to." Miss Irene took Faith in her arms. "Please don't cry, baby."

Faith buried her face in her mother's breasts as Miss Irene rocked her back and forth. It was just like when she and Hope were kids and scraped their knees or bruised their elbows. Miss Irene would rock them in her arms until they stopped crying and were ready to go out and face the world again. But she didn't want to go back out and face the world again. Not ever. She wanted to stay right there in her mother's arms and not think about Henry, not think about Hope, not think about the pain.

"Faith, sweetie, why don't I send Tina over to your house to get you some clothes so you can stay here with me for a little bit?" Miss Irene patted Faith on the back while she spoke. "In fact, how about you move back in here? The front room is vacant. Would you like that, baby? Would you like to come stay here with your mommy for a little while?"

The offer was tempting. There was nowhere else to stay. The apartment was in Henry's name since he was the only one old enough to sign a lease when they moved in. And who knows, he probably had Hope living there with him now. The thought made her head explode again, and she pulled away from her mother and buried her face in her hands, not crying, but simply rocking back and forth.

"You don't have to move in," Miss Irene said hurriedly, thinking she had offended Faith.

"No. It's not that. I just need to lie down, Mommy," Faith replied. "I'm not feeling up to—"

Both women jumped when they heard a knock on the door. "Who is it?" Miss Irene finally hollered.

There was no answer.

"I said, who is it?" Miss Irene hollered again.

"It's me, Miss Irene," Tina finally yelled back. "Why do you have your door locked?"

"Because I don't want anyone just bursting in here," Miss Irene mumbled under her breath as she unlocked the door and headed back into the room. "Lock it behind you again, Tina. Faith's not feeling well and I don't want her disturbed."

"What's wrong with her?" A man's voice demanded. Faith's mouth gaped open. It was Henry, pushing Tina out of the way as he strode toward her.

"Who said you could come in here?" Miss Irene demanded, blocking his path, her hands on her hips.

"I just came to speak to Faith." Henry tried to walk around Miss Irene, but the woman sidestepped along with him.

"She doesn't want to talk to you right now, Henry." She tried to push him back, but he wouldn't budge. He didn't push back either, he just stood over her and looked at Faith, who seemed paralyzed in the chair, unable to move or even talk.

"Faith, baby, we have to talk. I can explain everything. Just give me a chance," he pleaded.

"Tina, call the police," Miss Irene demanded, but to her astonishment Tina tucked the twenty dollars Henry had given her into her jeans pocket and slipped away.

"Get out of my house, right now, Henry Prince!" Miss Irene shouted as she pointed to the front door.

Henry navigated around Miss Irene and strode over to Faith's chair. He knelt down and took her hand. "Baby, I've been so worried about you." His voice cracked as he saw the circles under her eyes. "I've been looking for you everywhere, Faith. I've been calling everywhere trying to find you."

"She didn't want you to find her!" Miss Irene spat. She tugged at Henry's arm, trying to pull him up from the floor, but he ignored her.

"Baby, come on home with me so we can talk," he pleaded with Faith.

"There isn't anything to talk about," Faith said dully. "Everything that needs to be said has been said." She turned her head away as Henry's eyes filled with tears.

"A lot that's been said is lies and I can prove it," he said. "Hope! Get in here . . . now!"

Hope stepped into the apartment, head down, but Faith could see there was a large, white bandage over one eye. Oh, God, I hope I didn't take my sister's eye out, she thought as Hope slowly and silently walked toward her and Henry.

"Hope, you stay away from your sister," Miss Irene said through clenched teeth. "I mean it, you've already done enough damage." Miss Irene's face had turned beet red and a vein was bulging from her forehead.

"Mommy, please, just hear me out." Hope's lower lip was still bruised, and there were long scratches on the side of her face. "I'm not here to make trouble, I promise."

"Faith," Miss Irene turned to her other daughter, "do you want Hope in here?"

When Faith didn't answer, Henry started stroking her hand again. "Baby, just listen to what she has to say. Then, if you want me to leave, I will. But just give me a chance. Come on over here, Hope." Hope walked over and stood in front of Faith. "Now, start talking," Henry demanded. "And this time tell the truth."

"Faith, I lied. Me and Henry ain't do nothing." Hope's voice was firm, and she looked Faith straight in the eye as she talked. "I made a pass at him when he came in the room to wake me up, but he turned me down cold and said if I tried him again he was going to tell you. I got mad and wanted to get back at him for treating me so cold, so when you came in I made like we had made love, but we hadn't."

Faith's breath began to quicken as she looked back and forth between Henry and Hope. She wanted to believe them. Oh, God, she really wanted to believe them, but it just didn't make sense.

"Then why did it smell like sex? And, and . . ." her mind was racing, "what about the condom?" That's right. The damn condom. Let's see them try and explain that away.

Hope sighed and looked at Henry, then rolled her eyes at the ceiling. "Look, this is embarrassing, okay? I did have sex just a few minutes before you got there, but it wasn't with Henry."

"Tell her with who," Henry demanded.

"With old man Carpenter. The doorman guy."

"What?" Miss Irene interjected. "That old man that sits in the lobby? Why would you go to bed with him?"

"Because he offered her some crack." Henry explained. "They were smoking it in the guest room."

What do they take me for? Dumb? Faith leaned back in the chair, propped her face up on her elbow, and closed her eyes. "Oh, please. This is the stupidest nonsense I've ever heard. Why don't ya'll both just get up on out of here!" The story was so ludicrous that Faith actually started getting angry again. "The two of you couldn't come up with a better story than blaming it on poor Mr. Carpenter?" she asked Henry. "And you mean to tell me that you stood there and told me that lie because you wanted to get back at Henry? And you took that ass whipping I handed you and didn't change your story?" Faith shook her head. "Ya'll both better get out of my face."

"Faith, I swear to God." Henry raised his right hand in the air. "I swear on my mother's and sister's graves. Nothing happened."

"Mommy, would you please call the police?" Faith looked over at her mother.

"Wait, hold on one second!" Henry reached over and took the telephone from Miss Irene's hand. "Where's the telephone book? Someone get me the telephone book!" he said frantically.

"There shouldn't be too many Jeremiah Carpenters in here," Henry mumbled after Hope had found him the New York City white pages. "Shit, there's two. Okay, only one lives in Harlem." Henry started punching the buttons on the telephone.

"Hello? May I speak to Mr. Jeremiah Carpenter, please? . . . Mr. Carpenter, this is Henry Prince from apartment 2A. . . . I'm fine and you, sir? . . . Great. Was that your wife who picked up the telephone, sir? . . . Has she by any chance left the room? . . . Oh, good. Well, listen, the reason I'm calling is because Faith's sister told me what you guys were doing in the apartment last week. . . . No, I don't think you should hang up, Mr. Carpenter, I think you should let me finish what I have to say. The thing is, I'm going to put Faith on the telephone and I need you to tell her exactly what you and Hope did. Because if you don't, she's going to leave me. And if Faith leaves me, sir, I'm going to call back and tell Mrs. Carpenter just exactly what you wouldn't tell Faith. . . . Yes sir, I know, but right now I'm a desperate man and I'm willing to take drastic measures. . . . Hold on, one minute, sir, I'm going to put Faith on the telephone."

Faith's mouth was agape as Henry handed her the receiver. "Hello," she managed to croak.

"Listen, Miss Freeman," the voice was unmistakably Mr. Carpenter's, "I was up in your apartment smoking and carrying on with your sister last week. I'm sorry I disrespected you and your home like that. Now I gots to go." The phone went dead.

"See? Believe me now?" Henry was smiling, but tears were in his eyes as he reached his arms out to Faith. She jumped from the chair and rushed into them. "Baby, how could you ever think I would do something like that to you?" He stroked her hair as she cried softly.

"Henry, I'm so sorry. But how could I know she was lying?" Faith turned to Hope, who was standing in the corner of the room. "How could you try and hurt me like this, Hope?"

"Because she's a little slut," Miss Irene hissed. "She's miserable and she wants everyone around her to be just as miserable as her."

"Mommy, don't say that," Faith said, almost out of habit. She looked back at Hope, but her twin just shrugged her shoulders. Hope looked so pitiful standing there, her eyes looking down at the ugly green carpet, unable to look Faith in the eyes. Just like the afternoon when she and Papa were in Mommy's bedroom so long ago. Listening quietly while Papa tried to talk Faith out of telling. Saying nothing on her behalf. Saying nothing in her defense. Just standing there looking pitiful.

"No!" Faith pushed Henry away and walked over to Hope. "You've got to tell me why," she said quietly. "You've got to tell me why you went after Henry." Hope said nothing, just chewed her lip and looked down at the carpet. Faith grabbed her and started shaking her hysterically. "Why, Hope? Why? All I've ever done was try to help you. Why did you do this to me?"

"Faith," Henry tried to pry Faith's hands loose from her sister, "leave her alone and let's just go home. The two of you can talk later."

"Why, Hope?" Faith clung to her sister, who was now crying, but doing nothing to break free from her clutch. "Don't you know I love you? Don't you know I would do anything for you? Why would you do this to me? Why to me?"

"Faith, stop it!" Henry grabbed Faith, finally pulling her away.

"Don't you see that's why she did it? Because she knows how much you love her!"

"What? That doesn't make sense!" Faith sputtered. She looked back at Hope. "Why would you do it, Hope?" she screamed.

"Because I wanted to see if you would leave him," Hope started sobbing. "I wanted to see if you would leave him for me."

"What are you talking about?" Faith tried to run back to her sister, but Henry held her back.

"*Someone's got to choose me, don't they?*" Hope suddenly hollered. She shook uncontrollably as she looked around the room, at Miss Irene, at Henry, at Faith. "*Ain't I worth being the one that's choosed?*" she shouted.

"Hope . . ." Faith started toward her sister again.

"Stay away from me. I hate you." Hope started backing up. "I hate all of you!" She looked around the room again, then let out a howl that sounded like that of a wounded animal and suddenly ran out of the house.

"*Hope!*" Faith started to run out, but stopped when Henry suddenly yelled out.

"Faith! Oh my God! Call the paramedics!" Faith looked around to see her mother stretched out on the bed, gasping for breath. "I think your mother's having a heart attack!"

17

Reva Sinclair was there. So were Walter Frisby and all of the other clients of Freeman & Swanson Associates. Miss Irene was there, in the front row, fanning herself. The tiny room in St. Martin's church on Long Island was packed, and even the blaring air conditioner couldn't cool the air.

"Someone should have told Carol and Ann not to invite all these black folks," Hope grumbled as she adjusted the straps of her lavender bridesmaid dress in the dressing area upstairs. "They draw too much damn heat."

"Someone should have also told them they should try to make it to the church on time." Faith looked at her watch. "The wedding is supposed to start in thirty minutes and they haven't even arrived."

"Well, you kept on saying there wasn't going to be no wedding." Hope shrugged. "Looks like you might be right."

"Stand up and let me take another look at you, Baby Girl." Faith still couldn't get over how good Hope looked. Six months clean and putting on weight, her skin practically glowed. "Good Lord, you look beautiful."

"I don't feel beautiful. It's too damn hot in this dress," Hope grumbled. "You're lucky you're still in your slip."

Faith snorted. "Henry better hurry up over here with my dress. Can't you just see the maid of honor walking down the aisle in her underwear?"

"Hey, what did he get you for our birthday?"

"Just a rose and a card. He says he's going to give my real present later." Faith shrugged. "I know he'd better hurry and bring his butt over here so I can get dressed, though."

"He's here. He's right downstairs." Miss Irene struggled to catch her breath. "He asked me to come up and make sure you girls were okay. Said he'd be up in a minute." She sat down on the small sofa and started fanning herself. "Hope, sweetie, you look just beautiful."

"Don't I, Mommy?" Hope twirled around in front of the mirror. "I hate lavender, but this does look good."

"Come here and give your mother a hug." Miss Irene stretched out her arms.

"Don't mess up her hair, Mommy," Faith said as mother and daughter embraced. "Talk about beautiful, Mommy, you look great!" Faith exclaimed. "When did you get that dress?"

"Henry bought it for me." Miss Irene stuck out her chest. "He gave it to me this morning after he dropped you and Hope off at the church."

"It fits you perfectly, too," Faith said. "Mommy, you're going to have to quit losing weight or you're going to be smaller than your daughters."

"I guess the one good thing about having a heart attack is the diet they put you on." Miss Irene shrugged her shoulders, but the pride was evident in her voice. "I've already lost fifty pounds."

"And you look good, Mommy." Hope kissed her mother on the cheek.

"Not as good as you, baby." Miss Irene smiled.

"Shoot," Faith pouted, "everyone looks good but me. Hope do me a favor and run downstairs and tell Henry to hurry up."

"He's coming." Ann and Carol walked into the room arm in arm, both wearing tailored cream-colored linen dresses.

"Carol, you're not dressed yet!" Faith yelled. "Where's your dress?"

"It's coming," Carol giggled.

Faith looked at the two of them in disbelief. Carol had always been irresponsible, but Ann? Showing up late for her own wedding? *What the hell is going on?* she wondered.

"So, how does it feel to be an old married woman?" Hope playfully tapped Carol on the shoulder.

"I'm not married yet, girlfriend," Carol retorted. Ann smiled, but said nothing.

"Okay, the best man is here!" Henry carefully put the dress box down on the sofa next to Miss Irene. He was wearing a black tuxedo with a kente cloth tie and matching cummerbund.

"Honey, where are my clothes?" Faith asked after he kissed her on the cheek. "I've got to hurry and get dressed so I can help Carol on with her dress."

"Calm down, calm down, I've got your dress," Henry said quietly. "But you do look good just like this." He fingered the white satin slip lovingly, then kissed her on the cheek again. "Faith you're the most beautiful woman in the world, have I ever told you that? And I'm the luckiest man in the world to have you as my woman."

Faith smiled and caressed Henry's face. "Honey, look at you, you're sweating." She reached over and grabbed a tissue from the table and started wiping his forehead. "Are you okay?"

"I'm fine, baby. As long as you're here with me, I'll always be fine."

"Come on, ya'll. Stop with the mushy-mushy." Hope chuckled. "Ya'll act as if it was your wedding day and stuff."

"Oh, leave them alone," Miss Irene said amicably. "They'll get married when they're ready. I just hope I'm still alive to see it."

Henry stepped back from Faith and grinned. "You will be, Miss Irene. I promise."

"Hey," he started fumbling in his pocket, "you guys have got to look at this wedding ring."

"Ooh, Ann, that's so beautiful," Miss Irene exclaimed as Henry held the open ring box in front of her. "What is it? About three carats?"

"Ooh, Henry let me see," Faith tried to push Hope out of the way to get a glimpse.

"Hold on, Faith. I'm going to show it to you." Henry smiled, then pulled Faith to the middle of the room. "Here, take a look." He held the box in front of her, and then, to Faith's astonishment, sunk to one knee.

"Faith, we've been together fifteen years and they've been the most wonderful fifteen years that anyone could ever ask for," he said solemnly. "But I'm greedy, baby, and I'm asking for more. I'm asking you to spend the rest of your life with me."

Faith gasped, her hand flying to her mouth. Hope was squealing, and tears sprang to Miss Irene's eyes.

"Faith, you would make me the happiest man alive if you would consent to be my bride," Henry continued. "And I promise I'll make you the happiest woman alive."

"Oh, Henry," Faith's eyes were wet with tears and her voice quavered as she spoke, "I'm already the happiest woman alive, but of course I'll marry you, baby."

The room broke out in applause as the couple embraced.

"Well, when's the wedding day," Miss Irene asked after everyone had calmed down.

"Mommy, there's no rush—" Faith started.

"Today!" Henry said triumphantly. "Happy birthday!"

"Today?" Faith looked at Henry as if he had lost his mind. "We can't get married today. Ann and Carol are getting married today. And I don't have a dress or anything."

"No we aren't and yes you do." Ann walked over and pulled the wedding dress out of the box. "You didn't think it the least bit strange that Carol let *you* pick out her dress?"

"But, but, it was fitted for Carol," Faith stammered. "She and I don't wear the same size."

"It's your size," Carol piped in. "The dressmaker had to take your measurements for the bridesmaid gown, remember? She was really fitting you for the wedding dress."

"You mean, you guys aren't getting married?" Faith was struggling to catch her breath. Everything was going so fast.

"Us, getting married? Naw. In fact, we're breaking up," Carol chirped.

Faith's stare swung to Ann, but her partner just gave a half-smile and a slight shrug of the shoulders. "Don't worry, I'm fine. We can talk later."

"Yeah, anyway, Henry asked us to make believe we were so he could surprise you with all this," Carol continued.

Faith looked at Henry, standing there proudly, looking like the cat that had swallowed the canary. She turned to her mother and sister. "Did you two know about this, too?"

"Oh my God, no," Miss Irene croaked through her tears. "This is as much a surprise to me as it is to you."

"Me, too," Hope chimed in.

"I'm sorry, Mother Irene," Henry bent down and planted a kiss on her cheek, "but I knew if I told you you'd slip up and tell Faith. And I wanted it to be a surprise."

"Well, you could have told me," Hope said accusingly. She reached over and slapped Henry on the head. "I wouldn't have told Faith."

"I couldn't take the chance. My baby is one smart cookie." Henry grinned. He looked over at his watch and then at Faith. "Well, you'd better hurry up and slip into your dress. We don't want to keep our guests waiting too long, you know."

"Do the guests know?" Faith asked him.

"They will as soon as they see you walking down the aisle." Henry took Faith in his arms. "Faith, thank you for being in my life."